Margaret N. Germann
95 Autumnwood Dr.
Buffalo, NY 14227

W9-BEE-957

The Doctor
Rocks the Boat

The Doctor
Rocks the Boat

Robin Hathaway

THOMAS DUNNE BOOKS / ST. MARTIN'S MINOTAUR

NEW YORK

THOMAS DUNNE BOOKS.
An imprint of St. Martin's Press.

THE DOCTOR ROCKS THE BOAT. Copyright © 2006 by Robin Hathaway. All rights reserved. Printed in the United States of America. No part of this book may be used or reproduced in any manner whatsoever without written permission except in the case of brief quotations embodied in critical articles or reviews. For information, address St. Martin's Press, 175 Fifth Avenue, New York, N.Y. 10010.

www.thomasdunnebooks.com

www.minotaurbooks.com

Library of Congress Cataloging-in-Publication Data

Hathaway, Robin.
    The doctor rocks the boat / Robin Hathaway.—1st ed.
        p.   cm.
    ISBN-13: 978-0-312-34993-6
    ISBN-10: 0-312-34993-9
    1. Fenimore, Andrew (Fictitious character)—Fiction.
2. Physicians—Fiction.   3. Rowing—Fiction.   4. Fathers and sons—Fiction.   5. Congenital heart disease—Fiction.   I. Title

PS3558.A7475 D635   2006
813'.54—dc22

                                                      2006041715

First Edition: July 2006

10   9   8   7   6   5   4   3   2   1

To Bob,
who also rowed, and steered me on the right course

Smart lad, to slip betimes away
From fields where glory does not stay,
And early though the laurel grows
It withers quicker than the rose.

—A. E. HOUSMAN, "To an Athlete Dying Young"

ACKNOWLEDGMENTS

Without the help of the following people, this novel would not have been possible:

Robert Alan Keisman, M.D., a rower while in medical school, who shared his vast knowledge of both rowing and medicine.

Ruth Cavin, my editor and continual source of inspiration.

Laura Langlie, my agent and unfailing support.

Stephanie Patterson, social worker, who supplied insight into the problems of runaways and victims of child abuse.

Sara Jane Mitchell, whose knowledge of the history of Boathouse Row was very helpful.

Daniel Albert, a young rower who kindly provided me with current rowing data.

Julie Miller and Anne Keisman, trusted critics, who—even though close relatives—don't pull any punches!

The Doctor
Rocks the Boat

CHAPTER 1

In the early morning light, the Schuylkill River glowed with the luminosity of a pearl.

As Fenimore gazed from his train window, a dark speck glided onto the still surface. Was it an enterprising oarsman risen early to get in a few practice strokes before a big race? Or an ordinary citizen out for a recreational row? Fenimore had rowed for fun and relaxation when he was an intern, whenever he could fit it in, which wasn't very often. And his father had done so before him. It was the perfect antidote to the hectic rush of medical school. He remembered the bliss of rowing in a singles shell for all he was worth, then resting, raising his oars, and listening to the solitary *blip . . . blip . . . blip* of the water dripping off his oars into the river—as if it were the only sound on earth. Was there anything more peaceful than that? After a row, he would return to the chaos of the hospital feeling refreshed and ready to go.

Why had he stopped rowing? Why had he given up something he had enjoyed so much? Had life become that busy? Or was this just an excuse for pure, unadulterated sloth? Was life really worth living if you couldn't spend a few hours a week doing something you really loved? Nonsense. It was just a matter of discipline. He would stop by the Windsor Boat Club and renew his membership next week. As soon as he got back from this cardiology conference. He'd be damned if he'd lead a life of quiet desperation, like Thoreau described, with no joy in it. With the air of someone who has made an important decision, Fenimore shook open his *Inquirer* and began to read what evils the world had concocted while he was asleep.

On Monday, true to his word, Fenimore left the office earlier than usual and took a cab to Kelly Drive. The city was especially beautiful that spring afternoon. The cherry blossoms were in full bloom. And a haze of new green leaves, the color of pistachio ice cream, softened the trees along the Benjamin Franklin Parkway.

"Beautiful day," Fenimore ventured to the driver.

"Uh-huh" was his enthusiastic reply.

As the cab approached Boathouse Row, Fenimore's blood quickened. The sight of all those scantily clad young people jogging, biking, and Rollerblading along the river reminded him of his youth. *Hell, Fenimore, you aren't that old!* "Stop here, please," he told the cabbie.

The driver pulled over and stopped next to the Lincoln statue, which had been moved recently, Fenimore noted. It used to be in the center of Kelly Drive; now it was on the grass, over to one side. Where had he been when all this was going on? *Shut up in your stuffy office on Spruce Street,* he answered himself. He paid the cabbie and leapt out. "Keep the change!" he yelled and slammed the door with the vigor of a twenty-year-old.

While Fenimore waited for the traffic light to change—*That's new too,* he realized—he admired the row of elegant boathouses that lined the drive. They had always reminded him of a bunch of cheerful Victorian aunts. The one he was headed for had a peaked roof, brown shingles, a red door, and red trim. The Windsor Club had housed rowers and shells for more than 150 years. The Schuylkill Navy had been founded around 1860, he remembered, and except for a brief break during World War II, had been going strong ever since. His father had rowed at the Vesper Club before him. Not in competition, just for recreation. But when it came time for Fenimore to row, there was no place vacant at the Vesper Club, so he had joined the Windsor. The story of how his father began to row had become a family legend.

When Dr. Fenimore Sr. had been a resident at the Hospital of the University of Pennsylvania, or HUP, as it is more commonly called, he had lived in a stuffy rented room on a top floor. One sultry summer day, in search of a breeze, he had walked over to the river—and watched the rowers with envy. They had looked so cool and serene, despite the heat of the day, slicing calmly through the water.

On an impulse his father had knocked on the door of the first boathouse he came to. The Vesper Club. A handsome young man in shorts and nothing else threw open the door and said with an engaging grin, "Can I help you?"

Fenimore's father stared speechless for a moment as he recognized his greeter—the famous rower Jack Kelly Jr. "Uh . . . I was just wondering if . . . er . . . you ever rented shells to ordinary people?" he stuttered.

"Sure. What did you have in mind?" Kelly's blue eyes were so friendly and his manner so welcoming, Fenimore's father blurted his request: "I'm a resident over at HUP and things get pretty hectic. I just thought it would be nice to go out on the river—away from all the turmoil—maybe once or twice a week."

"Terrific idea." Again, that big grin. "When would you like to start?"

"Well, you better tell me what it costs first," his father said. "You see, residents don't get paid much and—"

"Ten dollars."

His father's face fell. Ten dollars a row, in the 1950s, was much more than a resident could afford.

Seeing his expression, Kelly said quickly, "That's the fee for a year's membership. You can row as often as you like. Unless there's a race going on, of course," he added half-apologetically.

His father was so stunned he could think of nothing to say.

"Come on in, I'll show you around." And the winner of the Diamond Sculls, that prestigious rowing award presented at Henley each year, treated Fenimore's father to a tour of the boathouse—in all its sweaty glory. He was showed the gleaming wooden shells, stored in their racks. They were all wood in those days. Carbo-fiber shells had yet to make their appearance. And the oars, standing in rows, like soldiers along the wall. He let down a singles shell and demonstrated to Dr. Fenimore Sr. how to launch it, and even assigned him a locker for his own use. As a result of that one impulse, his father rowed for more than twenty years, and introduced his son to the same pleasure when *he* was in medical school. There was one pleasure he couldn't share with his son, however. One day when his father had finished a row, there was a beautiful young woman, wearing a dress the color of apricots, standing on the dock. She was surrounded by young male admirers. When his father stepped onto the dock in a pair of skimpy shorts and nothing else, she turned. He stopped dead and stared. In those days, women were a rare sight at the boathouses.

Grace Kelly sent him a dazzling smile.

CHAPTER 2

Fenimore made his way through the throng of youths jogging in front of the Windsor Club and knocked on the door.

"Yes?" A heavyset man with a flushed face opened it. The face was familiar. Charlie Ashburn. An older fraternity brother from medical school, now an orthopedic surgeon at HUP, and a former rower of some skill. "Fenimore? For God's sake, where did you pop up from?"

"Hi, Charlie. I was just walking by and thought I'd try to renew my membership. Spring fever, I guess," he murmured.

"Come in. Come in. I'll sign you up." Charlie led him into an office that bore no resemblance to the one Fenimore remembered from earlier days—a cubbyhole under the stairs with a cluttered desk and a scruffy swivel chair. This office was spacious and air-conditioned, and the surface of the chrome desk was empty except for a miniature bronze replica of the Kelly statue—the original of which occupied a prominent place on Kelly Drive.

Ashburn unlocked the desk drawer and drew out a freshly minted application and a pen. "Sit right down and fill it out before you change your mind," he urged.

Fenimore scanned the sheet. The cost of membership had gone

up, but it was still a bargain. Fenimore filled out the form quickly and wrote a check. He handed it to Charlie.

Once the business was over, Charlie insisted on showing Fenimore around the club. "There've been a lot of improvements since your day, Fenimore." The upstairs, formerly a warren of lockers and furnished with a wooden bench or two, had been transformed into a grand ballroom for such functions as cocktail parties, wedding receptions, etc. "The revenue from renting space for these affairs helps keep dues down and the club afloat," Charlie told him. During the tour Fenimore tried to remember when he had last seen Ashburn. One year ago—or was it two?—at the Penn-Princeton football game. Afterward, back at the frat house, Charlie and his expensively clad wife had drunk too much and made snide remarks, not too discreetly, about some of the newer fraternity members. A few of the new recruits weren't up to the standards of *their* day, it seemed. Jennifer, Fenimore's constant companion, had also fallen under their scrutiny and failed their fashion test. She had committed the sin of not changing the sneakers and socks that she had worn to the game for the cocktail party. Most of the women had changed into panty hose and heels. "I could feel Caroline Ashburn's laser gaze searing my feet," she told Fenimore later.

"My son is starting as first stroke in the Ivy League Regatta this month," Ashburn told Fenimore proudly. They had paused in front of a wall of framed photographs of rowers from former days. Charlie pointed to a photo of a young man who looked as if he were in the last throes of cardiac arrest. "That's Chuck last year, after we won the Singles," Charlie said. "If he wins this year, he'll go to Henley."

"Congratulations." Fenimore remembered that Charlie had stopped rowing while still an undergraduate, although he had been an exceptional oarsman. Some health problem, he remembered vaguely. Charlie had been a patient of Fenimore's father at that time, and Fenimore remembered his father saying that he'd never seen a young man more devastated. He'd had his heart set on going to the Henley Regatta in England and winning the Diamond Sculls, one of the most coveted awards in rowing. Fenimore looked more closely at the picture of Charlie's son. His face was pallid and drained. Fenimore—renowned for his sixth sense in health matters—wondered if the boy's exhaustion was due to something more than the race.

Once Charlie started on his son, he couldn't stop. For the remainder of the tour, Fenimore heard every detail of every race Chuck had won. One thing Fenimore noticed was Charlie's recurring use of the word "we." He never said, "Chuck won that one." It was always, "We took that easily." Or, "That was a close one, but we did it."

While they were touring the upper level, Charlie heard someone enter the boathouse down below. He excused himself and went to see who it was. Shortly afterward, Fenimore heard voices raised in anger and a door slam. When Charlie came back, he was red-faced and puffing with indignation. "Would you believe? Some developer wants to 'reinvent' Kelly Drive," he said. "Get rid of the boathouses and turn this land into a modern marina!"

Fenimore was as outraged as Charlie. "Can they do that?" he asked. "Can't this site be registered as a historic landmark or something?"

"We're working on it," he said, frowning darkly. "But it isn't settled yet."

When Charlie had recovered, he drew Fenimore's attention to a shell stored high above the others. *The Zephyr* was the faded name on its bow. "Remember that?" he asked Fenimore. He did. Built before World War II of special woods imported from the Pacific Islands, it was the lightest shell in the club, and, for that reason, the most difficult to handle. Special oars had been custom made for *The Zephyr*—known as *The Zephyr Pair*. They were lighter than the others. Only the most skilled rowers were allowed to use this shell. "It should be called *The Ashburn*," Charlie said proudly. "It weighs only twenty-eight pounds—and Chuck's the only one who can handle her. He keeps his weight under one hundred and thirty and uses her for his singles races."

Not far from *The Zephyr* was a shell called *The Folly*. This had been Fenimore's favorite shell, and his father's before him. He was happy to see that it was still there. He couldn't wait to take it out, but it was too late today.

As they descended the broad staircase that had replaced the narrow, creaky one Fenimore remembered, he caught a glimpse of the river through the open doors.

"Like to see the view?" Without waiting for an answer, Charlie drew him out on the dock.

The smell of the river mixed with the scent of everything newly born—trees, grass, flowers—overwhelmed Fenimore. For a moment he forgot the ugly threats of the developer. The scents of spring don't move only the young. They have an even stronger effect on the middle-aged—stirring up waves of nostalgia for springs past as well as unleashing promises for the future. Fenimore couldn't wait to hit the water. If Ashburn hadn't been there he would have taken out a shell then and there.

"Quite a sight," Fenimore said, looking downriver, past the Water Works, toward the waterfall and the Philadelphia skyline beyond. He had always loved the skyline, and it seemed to grow better with the years. Although on a smaller scale, the tableau was almost equal to Manhattan's. At this time of day, the sun turned the sandy walls of that Greek edifice—the Art Museum—a dusky gold, the spare Rouse Building became a glittering column of silver, and City Hall took on the more subdued luster of an old pewter teapot.

"This was my favorite rowing time," Charlie said. "Then I'd come home and mix up a batch of martinis. Felt like I'd earned them after all that exercise."

"Dawn was my favorite time to row," Fenimore said. "Always got my day off to a good start."

Charlie glanced at his watch. "Say, the sun's over the yardarm. What d'ya say we run over to the league for a drink?"

Fenimore knew he was referring to the Union League, that prestigious club formed by Republicans during the Civil War.

"Thanks, Charlie, but I'll have to take a rain check. I have a date."

"Still single, eh?" Ashburn sent him a look tinged with envy.

Fenimore nodded, anxious to get away now. He hoped Charlie wasn't going to be the fly in the ointment of his future rowing plans. But he was pretty sure he would be long gone before Charlie showed his face at the Windsor Club. Dawn wasn't Charlie's thing.

It was such a beautiful evening, Fenimore decided to walk home. But as he strode down the Parkway, he couldn't get Charlie out of his mind. What was the health problem that had stopped him from rowing competitively? He had been his father's patient at that time—maybe his old records were still in the office. Fenimore had never gotten around to throwing out his father's files. Or, rather, he couldn't bring himself to do it. It would be like throwing his father out of his own office. He would look it up when he got back. He felt the new Windsor locker key in his pocket and stopped thinking about Charlie. Instead, he thought of gliding alone over the water in the early morning light, like the oarsman in that famous painting by Thomas Eakins. What was his name? Max Schmitt.

When Fenimore got home, he went straight to his office. His home and office were housed together in an old brownstone on Spruce Street. His office and waiting room occupied the front half of the first floor; the rest of the house served as his living quarters. He had inherited his father's house and medical practice when he died and had lived and worked there ever since. Fenimore was one of the few doctors left in Philadelphia who still practiced solo and made house calls. He knew he was a dying breed, and he didn't know how much longer he could hold out, working in such an old-fashioned way.

His father's case files were stored in a rusty cabinet in the corner.

The Ashburn file presented no difficulty. It was right where it should be—under *A*. He leafed through it, pausing at a report:

> Diagnosis—heart enlarged in the chest. X ray and the electrocardiogram suggested the heart muscle was thickened—and together with the episode of pre-syncope, the diagnosis appears to be hypertrophic cardiomyopathy.

Today an echocardiogram would make a more definitive diagnosis of the condition, but this report told Fenimore all he wanted to know. He read the note at the bottom, scrawled in his father's familiar hand. "This report confirms the finding that Charles Ashburn is predisposed to SCD (sudden cardiac death) and should not *under any circumstances* participate in competitive sports."

Fenimore sat down at his desk and stared at the report, now slightly yellowed with age. What was Charlie Ashburn's condition to him? His son Chuck could be perfectly fit. These conditions often skip a generation or disappear altogether, he reminded himself. *It's none of your business, Fenimore.* Snatching up the file, he stuffed it back in the cabinet.

CHAPTER 3

Fenimore had not been making it up—about having a date. He met Jennifer at eight o'clock to go to a movie that she had been dying to see.

"It's a romantic comedy," she told him in a mock-serious tone. "Just what you need."

"Why me?" he asked in all innocence.

"Because you're not romantic or comic," she said.

He denied this vehemently. "I'm the most romantic-comic person in Philadelphia since—"

"Since George Washington," Jennifer said, pulling a long face.

"No—since Ben Franklin. Now there was a romantic-comic fellow if there ever was one. He had all the ladies in Paris fawning over him and laughing at his jokes."

"Like you?" she said.

"Well, I have one Philadelphia lady fawn—"

"Dream on," she said hotly.

"Well—willing to go to the movies with me now and then," he amended. "Hey, I forgot to tell you what I did today," he said, changing the subject.

She looked interested.

"I rejoined the Windsor Club. I'm taking up rowing again."

She forgot her grievance and smiled at him. "That's wonderful. I thought you could use some exercise." Jennifer jogged every morning.

"What d'ya mean?" He looked down self-consciously at his slightly rounded paunch.

"Oh, nothing. But I really think it will be good for you to get back on the river. What made you decide to do it?"

"I was looking out the train window on my way to that cardiology conference in New York, and I saw this guy in a singles shell gliding over the water. Suddenly it all came back to me—how much I enjoyed rowing."

"Let's skip that movie and have a drink to celebrate," she said.

"Are you sure?" He looked pleased.

"Sure." She grabbed his arm and they took off for their favorite watering hole—the Raven. It was named after Poe's poem, even though it was nowhere near the famous author's house on Spring Garden Street. Tucked away on Samson Street, in the center of town, it was small and dark, with plenty of booths, but most important: It provided free snacks with the drinks. Fenimore ordered two glasses of Chardonnay. While they sipped and munched, he told her about running into Charlie Ashburn. "You remember him from that Penn-Princeton game?"

"Oh, yeah. His wife really gave me the once-over."

He told her about Charlie's aspirations for his son. "There's one problem." He set down his glass. "Charlie had a predisposition to sudden cardiac death. I looked up his old file. My father advised his parents that he avoid strenuous exercise and under no circumstances partake in competitive sports. As a result, Charlie dropped out of rowing at Penn. It was a body blow. I don't think he ever got over it." Fenimore took a deep swallow. "Now, he's fixed all his thwarted ambitions on his son who has inherited his father's rowing skills."

"Well, that's good, isn't it?" Jennifer said.

"Except for one thing—"

Jennifer looked up.

"His son may have inherited more than his father's rowing skills. He may have a predisposition to SCD too."

"Well . . . they must have had him tested."

"Maybe, but I think I should look into it."

"He's not your patient," Jennifer reminded him.

"No, but—"

"You feel responsible," Jennifer finished for him.

"Well, don't you think—"

"I guess you have no choice. I'm just . . ." she paused.

"What?" Fenimore prompted.

". . . afraid they won't thank you for your help."

He nodded. "You're probably right."

CHAPTER 4

When Mrs. Doyle, Fenimore's longtime nurse and office manager, came to work Tuesday morning, she thought the office was empty. But as she hung up her jacket and settled down at her desk, she heard strange sounds coming from Dr. Fenimore's inner office.

"Oomph! Arg! Oomph! Arg!"

She went over to the door and knocked gently. "Doctor? Are you all right?"

Heavy panting, followed by a weak, "Fine."

"You're sure?"

"Yes, sure." The voice was stronger and held a peevish note.

"All right, then." She went back to her desk and attacked the mound of paperwork that awaited her.

In a few minutes, the noises resumed. This time they were so agonizing she rushed to the door and shook the doorknob. "Doctor?"

Deep, heavy panting, followed by two gasped words, "What now?"

"Are you sure you're all right?"

He flung open the door and Mrs. Doyle was confronted by a sight that sent her blood pressure skyrocketing. Her employer stood before her red-faced, wearing nothing but a pair of yellow bathing trunks and brandishing a dumbbell.

"Oh!" She took a step back.

"Oh what? Haven't you ever seen a man in a bathing suit?"

"Yes. But not you," she said sharply.

"I'm getting in shape," he explained.

"For what? Your next patient? I hardly think Mrs. Dunwoody—"

"No, smarty-pants. I've rejoined the Windsor Club. I'm going rowing this afternoon."

Mrs. Doyle tried to suppress a smile.

"What's so funny? You think I'm too old?" He glared at her.

"Oh no. I was fifty when I took that refresher course in karate, but—"

"Well, then?"

"It's just—so sudden," she said lamely.

"You have to start sometime. No time like the present. He who hesitates is lost."

"Truer words were never said. Time waits for no man." Mrs. Doyle matched him homily for homily. "Speaking of which, your next patient is due any minute."

"Oh my. I have to shower. Keep her busy, Doyle." He hurried up the stairs just as Mrs. Dunwoody came in the front door.

"Was that the doctor?" she asked, her eyes fixed on his retreating naked back.

"Yes. He was up all night with an emergency. A cardiac arrest at . . . er . . . a swimming pool."

Mrs. Dunwoody's eyes were round. "A swimming pool—in the middle of the night?"

"Uh . . . yes. One of those all-night parties at a luxury hotel. The jet set, you know."

"Tch, tch. Poor man. When does he ever sleep?"

"Please have a seat," Mrs. Doyle said hastily. "We just got some new magazines—" To her great relief, the phone rang. It was Mrs. Lopez. She was calling to say that her son, Horatio, wouldn't be able to come to work that afternoon.

"What's the trouble?" asked Mrs. Doyle.

"A skateboard accident. He sprained his ankle."

"Has he had an X ray?"

"No . . ."

"Then how can you be sure it's just a sprain? Is it swollen?"

"Yes, but I've put ice on it and strapped it up."

"I'll tell the doctor. Meanwhile, tell him not to put any weight on it. I'll call you back in a few minutes."

When the doctor reappeared, to Mrs. Doyle's relief, he was dressed in his usual white shirt, navy suit, regimental striped tie, and oxfords. She told him about Horatio.

"Did you tell him to get an X ray?"

"Yes, but Mrs. Lopez doesn't have a car, you know, and they really can't afford a cab."

"Well, call her back. Tell her I'll be over as soon as I finish here and take him to the ER."

"Yes, Doctor."

"Mrs. Dunwoody . . ." Fenimore beckoned.

"I hear you were up all night with that jet set," she said.

"Er . . ."

Mrs. Doyle sent him a covert wink.

"That's right. Never a dull moment."

"You doctors lead such hard lives, I always say—" The door closed on what she always said.

The phone rang again and two more patients came in the front door. Another morning at Dr. Fenimore's office was in full swing.

CHAPTER 5

Fenimore rang the bell beside the door of a small row house in South Philadelphia. He had been instrumental in finding this brick house for Horatio and his mother and had helped them to acquire a fair mortgage. He had offered to help finance the mortgage, but Mrs. Lopez had flatly refused. "We can manage," she told him. Before that, they had lived at the Morton Towers—a concrete public housing complex.

Mrs. Lopez opened the door. "Doctor, this is so kind."

Her blue eyes and fair skin always startled Fenimore. Irish to the core, her son looked nothing like her. Horatio had dark hair and a complexion like strong tea—the image of his father, who was of Spanish background. But Mr. Lopez was long gone, the victim of a random shooting on his front step when his son was four.

"Not at all," said Fenimore. "How's the patient?"

She led him past the offending skateboard that leaned against the wall, into the small living room. Fenimore's teenage employee was happily ensconced on the sofa in front of the TV, a glass of orange juice and a half-eaten donut resting on a table within easy reach.

"Hi, Doc." He grinned. "Sorry I can't get up." He glanced at his ankle, neatly strapped with adhesive tape.

Fenimore bent to examine the injury. When he squeezed the ankle gently Horatio winced. "Well, you'll have to get up if you're going to make it to my car. Your mother and I will give you a hand." He crooked his finger at Mrs. Lopez. "Put one arm around my neck," he ordered Horatio, "and the other around your mother's, and hop."

Horatio obeyed. In this manner the threesome made its way out to the curb. The front steps were a major obstacle, but with the help of the railing the boy managed to gain the sidewalk without mishap. He stretched out on the backseat with a dramatic groan. Mrs. Lopez slipped into the passenger seat, and Fenimore drove.

The hospital was only a ten-minute ride. Once there, Fenimore fetched a wheelchair from the ER for his patient and brought it out to the car. Horatio seemed to be enjoying his invalid status, especially when a petite, blond nurse came up and made a fuss over him.

"Poor boy. What happened?" she asked with a concerned smile.

Horatio gazed up at her and said dolefully, "Skateboard."

Her smile vanished. "You crazy kids! Deliberately setting out to break your necks. I have no sympathy for you." She spun away.

Horatio stared after her. "She's obviously never surfed," he said to no one in particular.

Fenimore wheeled him into the ER, closely followed by Mrs. Lopez.

The X ray revealed that Horatio's ankle was not sprained but broken in three places.

Two hours later, Horatio exited the ER, deftly wielding a new pair of crutches, his left foot in a cast. Compared to skateboarding, crutches were child's play. His mother followed behind, wearing a look of weary resignation. Fenimore, who had used the time efficiently to visit his hospital patients, reappeared at the hospital entrance in his car just as mother and son emerged.

"Perfect timing!" he sang out, throwing open the front and back doors. "Shall I drop you at school, Rat?" Fenimore asked, slyly. "You still have a few hours."

"Hell, no—"

"*Ray!* Watch your mouth."

Ray was Mrs. Lopez's pet name for her son, but the boy preferred to be called Rat.

"Sorry, Doc, but I've got this great excuse to stay home today, and—"

"If it wouldn't be too much trouble, Doctor"—his mother cut in—"the school is only a few blocks from our house."

"Aw, geez . . ."

"But we better stop at the house first and pick up his book bag. It has his homework in it."

"Holy sh—"

"*Ray!*"

Grumbling continued intermittently from the backseat until the bag was picked up and the school was in sight.

As Fenimore helped the boy out, Horatio grimaced.

"Did they give you anything for the pain?" he asked.

"They gave me a prescription." Mrs. Lopez produced it from her purse.

"I'll get it filled and deliver it to the school nurse," Fenimore said. "You can pick it up in about an hour at the infirmary, Rat."

"No, Doctor. You've done enough," Mrs. Lopez said. "I'll take care of this. There's a drugstore right around the corner."

"But you have to get to work."

"So do you," she said firmly and waved him on.

"Thanks, Doc!" Horatio yelled after him, and his mother thought maybe there was some hope for her son after all.

CHAPTER 6

When Fenimore returned to his office, he glimpsed the back of an elegantly clad, expensively coiffed woman in his waiting room. He was annoyed. He thought he was done for the day. He had planned to leave the office early and head for the river. In a whisper, he asked Mrs. Doyle to identify the interloper.

"A Mrs. Ashburn," she said. "She apologized for coming without an appointment. She seemed upset."

Fenimore quickly swallowed his resentment and entered the waiting room. "Caroline?"

She turned abruptly. "Oh, Andrew, I'm sorry to barge in on you like this, but—"

"Come in. Come in." He guided her into his inner office and, much to his nurse's discomfiture, closed the door.

When Caroline was seated, Fenimore said, "I saw Charlie yesterday."

"I know. That's why I'm here. When he mentioned seeing you, it occurred to me that you were the one person who might be able to help."

"In what way?"

"It's my son, Chuck."

20

"Is he ill?"

"No. At least"—she looked at Fenimore—"not yet. But he will be if someone doesn't stop him."

"Stop him?"

"From rowing," she said sharply. "That's all he and my husband think about, day and night: 'Row, row, row your boat . . .' They drive me crazy."

"But it is a fine sport—"

"Is it?" Her harsh tone cut Fenimore off like a chain saw. "Do you call it fine when someone gets up at four o'clock in the morning, every morning, and drives himself to such a state of exhaustion he can barely row back to the boathouse, then arrives for his first class in a state of near collapse to put in a full academic day, only to go back on the river to row another two hours, then is up until midnight hitting his books, only to rise at four o'clock the next morning—and repeat the whole process again the next day for five days a week? And on the weekends, of course, there are the races!"

"But—"

"*But?*"

"If he's been in training, his body should be used to this regimen."

"No body is used to that regimen, Andrew. It's—it's cruel."

To Fenimore's surprise, her eyes brimmed with tears. This was more than a simple case of an overprotective mother, he decided.

"Has Chuck complained to you?"

"Oh God no. He wouldn't dare. He'd be afraid his father would get wind of it. You see, ever since Chuck was about ten years old, Charlie has had his heart set on his son going to Henley and winning the Diamond Sculls."

Fenimore's eyes widened.

"Yes, I know. It's insane. But Charles had to quit rowing when he was Chuck's age because of a heart defect. Your father was the one who made the diagnosis. Now he's trying to make up for it by killing his son—"

"Whoa. Those are pretty strong words. Why should this kill Chuck?"

Caroline's eyes narrowed, destroying all the beneficial effects of carefully applied cosmetics. "Chuck may have the same defect Charlie has."

"You've had him examined?"

She shook her head.

"Why not? It's easy to find out—"

"Charlie discouraged it. He said, 'That was all long ago.' And Chuck didn't want an exam. . . ."

"But surely, in this case . . ."

She gave a short, mirthless laugh. "You don't know Charlie. On the surface, he seems affable, but underneath he's a steel rod. When he wants something, he gets it, whether in business, in marriage"—she paused infinitesimally—"or sports. And Chuck takes after him."

Fenimore tried to absorb this. After a moment he said, "How can I help?"

"As I said, your father diagnosed Charlie when he was at Penn."

Fenimore nodded.

"Do you have a record of that diagnosis?"

"I'd have to check," he hedged. "It was a long time ago."

"Charlie never went back to your father after that. It would have been too painful." She bit her lip.

"I still don't see—"

"Charlie wants to ask you for dinner. I thought when you come"—She assumed there was no question of his *not* coming— "you could ask him if he's had Chuck examined. Explain that sometimes this defect can be inherited."

"This isn't something I usually discuss over dinner."

"Make an exception!" Caroline's eyes flashed.

Fenimore waited for her to calm down.

"Sorry, Andrew." She brushed a strand of hair from her eyes. "But we're talking about a matter of life and death."

"You're talking about a matter of life and death."

"But there is a risk. You implied so yourself."

"The first thing is to have Chuck examined."

"I have a plan." She leaned forward. "During dinner you could mention that while cleaning out your office you came across Charlie's old record and you wondered if Chuck had been examined recently. Mention that sometimes these defects are inherited."

"This is highly unprofessional—"

"Let me finish. I'm going to invite a lot of Charlie's most influential friends to this dinner. Windsor's president, the rowing coach, even Chuck's biggest rowing competitor—Hank Walsh and his father, Henry. They're black, you know. A first for the Club." She let him in on this big news. "And they will all hear what you have to say. If it becomes public knowledge that Chuck should have this exam, Charlie won't dare refuse. Charlie is determined, but he is also very sensitive to public opinion."

Fenimore was silent. Finally he said, "Let me think about it."

"We don't have much time."

"How's that?"

"The big regatta, the one that determines who goes to Henley, takes place at the end of the month. This period is especially hard on the rowers. The training is very rigorous. I want to spare Chuck that, if possible. I've noticed that he's been flagging lately. When he gets home at night he . . . he looks like death warmed over."

"He still lives at home?"

"Oh yes. So Charlie can keep an eye on him. Make sure he does his exercises and is on time for every practice."

"That's quite a commute from Bryn Mawr."

"Charlie drives him in most mornings."

Fenimore stroked his chin. "Let me sleep on it," he said, "and I'll let you know tomorrow."

Resigned but not happy, Caroline rose. Before leaving, she turned. "Have you ever read A. E. Housman?" she asked.

Fenimore frowned. "I think I had to memorize one of his poems. Something about cherry trees . . ."

"Well, refresh your memory and try 'To an Athlete Dying Young.'"

As Fenimore ushered Mrs. Ashburn out, Mrs. Doyle observed them from behind her desk. When the doctor returned, she pretended no interest in his last patient, but she didn't fool Fenimore. Her curiosity crackled through the office like static electricity.

"For your information, Doyle, that was not a patient. Just a friend with a family problem."

"I see."

Too late for a row now, he returned to his inner office, deep in thought.

Later, after eating a meager supper of tuna on rye washed down with a Coke, Fenimore trudged up to the attic. When he stepped inside, he was met with the scents of old things stored too long in an airless space. The last of the sun's rays filtered through the single dirty window, endowing the accumulated clutter with a golden hue and turning the dust motes into flecks of gold. The room was crammed with cartons and suitcases, broken lamps and worn-out pieces of furniture. *Why do we hang on to these things?* he wondered. *Are we too lazy to sort them out and get rid of them? Or does it go deeper than that? If we dispose of these things from the past, are we afraid we will diminish ourselves in some way? Enough introspection, Fenimore.* He headed for the corner where he thought his old school books were stored. *There they are!* He spied four cartons labeled in his mother's precise hand: MEDICAL SCHOOL, COLLEGE, HIGH SCHOOL, CHILDHOOD. He pulled the one labeled HIGH SCHOOL toward him and tore it open. The first thing he saw were his report cards, neatly tied together with string. *Good old Ma! She had been proud of me, hadn't she?* He devoted a few moments to her memory. A brave woman, she had left her home in Prague to come to this country and marry a man who spoke not a word of her native language. Raised two sons and made a life for herself in Philadelphia. On the whole, she had seemed content, sinking only occasionally into sad moods, which Fenimore now suspected had been bouts of simple homesickness. He didn't think much of visiting graves. He felt much closer to his mother here in the attic, where she had lovingly packed up his books and papers than at Laurel Hill Cemetery overlooking the Schuylkill, where she was buried. Immortality was a funny thing; people lived on in the oddest ways. He had a girlfriend long ago who died in a car crash. Sara. She had taught him how to cook spaghetti. "I can never keep it from sticking," he had told her. "Oh, that's easy," she'd said and sprinkled a few drops of olive oil in the water. Now, every time he made spaghetti and added oil to the water, he thought of Sara. That was true immortality.

He laid the report cards aside. He knew what they contained. Straight As. Except for that one semester when he had been in love and slipped to a B+ in geometry. He still shuddered at the cause of this black mark on his record. Franny had turned out to be not only fickle but *stupid*! *Maybe that's why we become pack rats,* he thought. *We hate to sort through our stuff and be reminded of our past foibles.* He lifted the next item. A notebook labeled, in Fenimore's own boyish hand, AMERICAN HISTORY—McDOUGAL. He remembered McDougal fondly. A superb teacher who sprinkled his lectures with humorous anecdotes to help weld knowledge to the minds of the most lackluster students. He moved on. "Ah!" He came upon the volume he was looking for, *Snyder and Martin,* the well-worn collection of English literature he had treasured. Chaucer, Donne, Shakespeare—on to Keats, Coleridge, Browning. Seated on the carton labeled COLLEGE, Fenimore browsed in the fading light. He had read most of *The Ancient Mariner* when he gave a start, remembering why he was there. He quickly searched out Housman, and in the gathering dusk, read the poem Caroline had recommended. One verse struck him as particularly poignant.

> *Smart lad, to slip betimes away*
> *From fields where glory does not stay.*
> *And early though the laurel grows*
> *It withers quicker than the rose.*

Fenimore tried to remember being Chuck's age. His dreams and aspirations. They had been very different. To be a doctor had been his all-consuming desire. A somewhat more substantial dream than winning a race. One that would last a lifetime, not disappear in a flash of oars. He remembered those athletes who bloomed so young; everything that came after seemed an anticlimax. Paul Newman had portrayed such a fellow to perfection in *Cat on a Hot Tin Roof*. The agony and futility of jumping hurdles when his body could no longer respond to his call. Even Elizabeth Taylor, with all her charms, could not interest this former football star.

Surely Chuck could replace his insubstantial dream with another, longer-lasting one, Fenimore told himself.

By the time he left the attic, it was so dark he had to feel his way to the door like a blind man.

CHAPTER 7

Two days later Charlie invited Fenimore to dinner. And Fenimore accepted.

"Bring your girlfriend," Charlie urged. "Caroline's asking a big crowd. Why, on such short notice, I don't know. But once a woman gets an idea in her head . . ." He made a circular motion with his finger next to his temple. When he was with Charlie, Fenimore wasn't sure there had ever been a feminist revolution.

"Thanks, I will," Fenimore said, referring to Jennifer, and wondered what her reaction to the invitation would be. He found out that evening.

"Oh lord. Do I have to wear a dress?"

"Well, I imagine—"

"All those overstuffed matrons will be decked out in their Talbots suits and Banana Republic sundresses."

Fenimore had never thought about where Jennifer bought her clothes. He himself leaned toward thrift shops and the Salvation Army stores. "If you'd rather not . . ." he began.

"Oh no. I'll go. After all you've told me about the Ashburn family, I'm dying of curiosity. I'll dig up something to wear."

·   ·   ·

Fenimore drew up to the curb on Walnut Street, in front of Nicholson's Bookstore. Jennifer and her father owned and lived above the store and because of the parking problem, she often waited for him on the sidewalk. He almost didn't recognize her. Instead of her usual jeans and T-shirt, she was dressed in a white linen top, a long lavender print skirt, and white sandals. She looked stunning. Two men who were passing by bestowed admiring glances on her as she stepped into the car. Fenimore wondered fleetingly why she didn't dress up more often, but quickly banished the thought as being politically incorrect or worse—disloyal.

"You look smashing," he said.

"And you sound like Bertie Wooster." Jennifer made a face.

"I've always fancied myself as Jeeves," Fenimore said.

"Dream on."

"You're in a fine mood."

"Sorry. I guess it's the thought of mingling with all those matrons."

"Some matroons will be there too."

"Matroons?"

"Mates of the matrons."

"You made that up."

It was rush hour, so the drive to Bryn Mawr via the Schuylkill Expressway was slow. As they crawled along, parallel to the river, Fenimore pointed out Boathouse Row. "Look, the lights just came on!"

He referred to the beads of lights that outlined the boathouse walls, peaked roofs, windows, and doors, transforming the Victorian dowagers into a row of homes from Loony Tunes. He half expected Elmer Fudd to step out on one of the docks, bearing a shell on his head.

"They are fabulous, aren't they?" Jennifer agreed. "Have you been rowing yet?"

He nodded. "Twice. But I'm still afraid to go at dawn. I thought I'd better go when other rowers are around in the beginning—in case I have an accident and someone has to rescue me."

"But it's not as if you're a novice," she said. "Doesn't the skill come right back—like ice-skating or bicycling?"

"Up to a point. But you still have to be careful. Once, someone tipped over and went right over the falls."

"Good grief. What happened to him?"

"He was battered to a bloody pulp on the jagged rocks below."

"Do you have to be so graphic?"

"Sorry." He slid a disc into the CD player and they listened to Mozart the rest of the way.

Charlie Ashburn made a good income as chief of orthopedics at HUP, and Caroline was heir to one of Philadelphia's foremost pharmaceutical firms. After entering their drive, flanked by two concrete lions, it took some time before they caught sight of the mansion. The parking area to one side of the grandiose granite pile already held a Porsche, a BMW, various Cadillacs, and a Lexus SUV. Fenimore parked his 1997 Chevy next to the Porsche. He could afford a better car but had no desire for one. "If it runs, that's all that matters" was his philosophy. Once, after a trip to a similar affluent neighborhood, a township police car had followed his shabby vehicle to the county line, and Fenimore was convinced the cop had suspected him of casing the neighborhood for future heists.

"Andrew! How nice." Caroline greeted him with a peck on the cheek. "And this is . . . ?"

"Jennifer."

Jennifer forced a smile.

"Jennifer . . . ?" She paused, waiting for a last name. In Ashburn circles, people still supplied their surnames, to make it easier to determine the person's social origins, Fenimore surmised.

"Nicholson." Jennifer supplied hers, grudgingly.

"Come in and join the party!" Charlie appeared behind his wife. "You're the last, I think." Casting an appraising glance at Jennifer, he asked, "What would you like to drink?"

He seemed put out by their orders for two white wines. He was a martini and bourbon man himself, he said. "Acquired the taste in college, and never gave it up." He laughed.

Fenimore scanned the room. True to her word, Caroline had assembled an august group. He recognized Ted Oldfield, president of the Windsor Club. A dapper, friendly fellow, he sported a small moustache. And the Windsor coach, Frank O'Brien, was holding court, surrounded by a circle of admiring young men and women—primarily rowers. Today, there were as many women rowers as men. Short and muscular, O'Brien had been first stroke for Windsor at one time and his reputation in the world of rowing was legendary.

When Charlie returned with their drinks, he had his son, Chuck, in tow. The slender, taciturn youth stayed only long enough to be introduced, then rejoined the group gathered around his coach.

On the other side of the room, Fenimore was surprised to see Cornelius Wormwood, head of the Philadelphia Planning Commission. Charlie explained that they hoped to persuade him to vote against the *horrid* marina when the proposal came up next week. He pointed out two other key figures in the marina saga— Jack Newborn, the developer, and William Ott, the chief architect. They were engaged in a conspiratorial conversation in a corner of the living room. Newborn's squat figure radiated a fierce energy, while Ott's spaghetti-like form oozed lassitude as he lounged against the mantelpiece. The Ashburns, it seemed, had no objection to mixing with the enemy.

Two dark, lean men hovered on the sidelines, talking to each other. One in his fifties, the other about twenty. The Walshes, father and son, Fenimore decided. The son looked ill at ease, but the father seemed relaxed. O'Brien had been instrumental in getting the younger Walsh into the club, overcoming some initial resistance, Caroline told Fenimore. But Hank had proved an excellent choice. He was the only rower who could compete with her son, Chuck.

"Henry Walsh, Hank's father, is a lawyer at Williams, Benner, and Dunn—a very prestigious firm," Charlie informed them in a low voice as he brought their drinks. "Hank is Chuck's only serious competitor. We have to keep our eye on him."

"I'd like to meet them," Fenimore said.

Charlie led Fenimore and Jennifer over to the two men.

"Want to lay odds on tomorrow's race, Charlie?" Henry Walsh spoke in a joshing tone.

"You know it's illegal to bet on amateurs," Charlie said stiffly. "This is Andrew Fenimore—a cardiologist—and Jennifer . . . ?"

"Hi." Jennifer stuck out her hand, and they shook all around.

Jennifer asked young Hank how he had become interested in rowing, and Fenimore listened to Henry Walsh and Charlie banter about their sons' prowess. Charlie's jibes had more of an edge than Henry's, Fenimore thought. A tall, distinguished stranger with a British accent joined their group and injected an occasional snide remark.

Fenimore and Jennifer had barely finished their wine when the party was summoned to dinner. Caroline wasn't wasting any time getting to the purpose of the gathering, Fenimore noticed. It was quite a trek from the living room to the dining room. In size, the rooms equaled those of the art museum on the Parkway, and the furnishings were probably worth about the same.

The party consisted of twelve. (Fenimore counted.) He had been seated on the left side—in the center—so everyone could easily hear him when it came time for him to play his part. Caroline and Fenimore had decided that the lull between the entrée and dessert would be the best time for his performance. Mellowed by food and drink, the guests would be receptive, and, having worn out earlier topics of conversation, eager for new material.

The Brit was seated on Fenimore's right. He introduced himself as Geoffrey Hunter-Powell, from Oxford. "I'm in the States for one reason," he said with a deprecating smile. "To scout out your rowers."

Fenimore looked at him with new interest. "What do you think of them?"

"Oh, top-hole," he said jovially. "But they'll lose, of course."

"We did win a few when Kelly was around," Fenimore reminded him.

"True," the Englishman allowed, "but those days are long gone." His smile failed to take the sting out of his words.

Fenimore turned to the person on his left—a sturdy, freckle-faced woman.

"Jill O'Brien," she said with a smile.

"The coach's wife?"

She nodded.

"What's it like being wedded to a river rat?" Fenimore asked.

She laughed. "I *am* a bit of a sailor's wife, but we have a house full of kids and I don't have much time to miss Frank."

"Are they all rowers?"

"Well, they're all under ten, so it's a bit early to tell. But I'd put my money on Beth, our oldest daughter. She's a good little athlete and women rowers have finally come into their own."

"Time marches on," Fenimore said, remembering Jack Kelly Sr. being refused entry in the Henley race because he was a mere tradesman. He owned a successful brick business but lacked a university education. Kelly had been so outraged by this snub, he had sent his jockstrap to the king. Fenimore was glad that times had changed and Beth O'Brien would not have to send her bra to Queen Elizabeth II!

The grapefruit and chicken breast courses passed uneventfully, except for one minor incident. Frank O'Brien looked over at Chuck, who was seated across from him, and said brusquely, "Better hit the sack early tonight."

Chuck had not contributed much to the conversation, but Fenimore wasn't sure whether this was due to shyness or fatigue. The boy merely nodded in response to his coach. Caroline, seated at the head of the table, overheard the remark and her bright hostess façade faded momentarily.

When the dishes were cleared, a dark-skinned woman in a white uniform circled the table, taking orders for coffee—regular or decaf. When she disappeared into the kitchen, Caroline glanced at Fenimore. With a start, he realized this was his cue.

At the first break in the general conversation, Fenimore spoke up. "Funny thing happened today, Charlie," he said, staring down the table at his host.

Charlie looked at him, expecting a joke.

"I was cleaning out some of my father's old files and came across a medical report of yours."

Charlie's smile faltered.

"I was reminded of why you gave up rowing."

The silence at the table was as complete as at a Quaker meeting—undisturbed by a single cough, murmur, or clink of silverware.

"I assume Chuck has been tested for SCD?" Fenimore ended his statement with a question mark.

Charlie rolled his eyes. "Well, actually I'd sort of forgotten about all that."

O'Brien cast a quick glance at Chuck, but his expression was unreadable.

The Walshes exchanged a puzzled look.

The others stirred restlessly. One guest looked over his shoulder, as if in search of the dessert.

"Well," Fenimore went on, "I'd certainly look into it. With a genetic history like yours, you can't be too careful." Fenimore's own heart was on the verge of fibrillating. Charlie's face had turned crimson, his jaw was clenched, and Fenimore knew if they had been alone, he would have been dead meat. Aware of the tension, Jennifer reached for his hand under the table and squeezed it.

"I'll look into it." Charlie threw his napkin on the table and left the room.

Chuck stared after his father and started to rise. Caroline stopped him. "Dear, would you go in the kitchen and see what's keeping the strawberries. I think they must have strayed back to the store."

A stream of relieved laughter flowed around the table.

Reluctantly, Chuck headed for the kitchen.

Slowly the general conversation resumed and the strawberry shortcake made its belated appearance. Charlie's chair remained empty through dessert, coffee, and the liqueurs. Fenimore and Jennifer excused themselves as soon as dinner was over. Pale but triumphant, Caroline accompanied them to the door. "Thank you, Andrew," she said. Her words were simple but heartfelt.

Once in the car, Jennifer said, "Well, that was a nice, relaxing evening."

Fenimore tried to explain why he had ignored medical ethics and discussed a patient's private affairs at a dinner party. He thought Jennifer, of all people, would understand about the Housman poem. When he finished, she was silent for so long, he wasn't sure what she thought.

"I knew you couldn't resist," she said at last, "but I'm not happy about it. Did you see Ashburn's face when he left the room?"

Fenimore nodded.

"If looks could kill . . ."

CHAPTER 8

In the hectic pace of his cardiology practice, Fenimore didn't give a thought to the Ashburns and their problems for several days. But on Wednesday afternoon his workload became lighter, and Fenimore decided to head for the river. As he entered the Windsor Club around four thirty, he remembered this was Charlie's favorite time to hang out, and he looked around warily.

But the only people in sight were a group of youths hauling in an eight-oared shell, amid a lot of good-natured shouting and kidding. Fenimore moved out of their way and climbed to the third floor, where the lockers were located. While changing into shorts and a T-shirt, he wondered if his performance at the Ashburn party had brought any results. He had heard nothing from Caroline. *Heck, I didn't come here to worry about the Ashburns. I came here to relax and enjoy myself.*

He shoved the shell into the water and carefully stepped in. It rocked and dipped precariously as he settled into the seat. A singles shell is a delicate instrument. Made of light carbo-fiber, it weighs only about thirty pounds and is easily tippable. He slipped his feet into the open shoes anchored to the bottom, fastened the

Velcro straps, and reached for the oars. Facing the stern and the city skyline, he fit the oars into the oarlocks. Then, with deft strokes, he began to propel the craft upstream, toward the Falls Bridge.

Catch. Drive. Recover. Finish. The four parts of the rowing cycle came back to him. Adopting an easy rhythm (he was here to relax, not to prove his skills), he slid slowly under the Girard Avenue Bridge, past the Grant statue and Peter's Island on his left. All troublesome thoughts were either wafted away by the gentle breeze or carried downstream by the flow of the river.

When he reached the Columbia Avenue Bridge, he turned reluctantly and headed homeward. A pair of Canada geese floated across his path, seemingly unaware of his presence. A seagull swooped overhead. *You're a long way from home, buddy.* (The Atlantic Ocean was a good sixty-five miles from Philadelphia.)

As Fenimore pulled up to the dock, the skyline was a mix of glittering silver and tawny gold. After successfully lifting the shell out of the water, he paused to catch his breath and take in the splendid view.

"Have a good row?"

Fenimore turned. Charlie Ashburn stood on the dock behind him. Something about his stance, his tone, his expression, caused Fenimore to move instinctively away from the edge of the dock.

"Yes. It was fine." Fenimore started to hoist the shell onto his shoulders.

"Let me give you a hand." Charlie, a much bigger man than Fenimore, raised the shell as if it were made of straw and carried it effortlessly into the shed.

"Thanks." Fenimore followed him.

When the shell was safely secured in the bay, Charlie said, "Chuck had that exam you recommended. Got a clean bill of health."

"That's great," Fenimore said sincerely. "Where did you take him?"

"No place you've ever heard of. A hospital upstate. Friend of mine's head of cardiology there. Former classmate. I respect his judgment."

Fenimore caught the implication—Charlie didn't think much of Fenimore's judgment. "Well, I'm certainly glad everything turned out so well." He started for the stairs to the locker room, but Charlie remained in the way.

"I was a little surprised at your bringing up my medical history at dinner, Fenimore. Isn't there such a thing as patient privacy anymore?"

Fenimore felt the blood rush to his face. "Sorry if I was indiscreet. It was a case of intellectual curiosity outweighing social propriety, I'm afraid."

Charlie still didn't move. "If I remember rightly, as a resident you were a stickler for propriety."

"Was I? Quite the prig, I guess." He laughed. "Now if you'd let me pass, I'd—"

Charlie didn't budge. His eyes narrowed and he placed a large open hand against Fenimore's chest. "Keep out of my family affairs, Fenimore."

As Fenimore stared, the man gave him a shove that sent him staggering backward. Regaining his balance, Fenimore said nothing.

Charlie left him standing there.

As Fenimore made his way shakily upstairs to his locker, he wondered when a nice Main Line boy like Charlie had adopted Mafia manners. And, more important, why?

When Fenimore returned to his office, there was a phone message waiting for him from Caroline Ashburn. He'd had his fill of the Ashburns. Reluctantly he returned her call.

"Oh, Andrew, I have the most wonderful news. Charlie took Chuck to be examined and he's fine! Not a sign of Charlie's old trouble. And I owe it all to you. I can't thank you enough."

"I'm very happy," Fenimore said. "Where was the exam done?"

"At Pine Lake Hospital in the Poconos. A friend of Charlie's, Dan Burton, lives and practices up there. He and Charlie hunt together a lot. Sometimes they take Chuck along."

"This may seem like a strange request, Caroline, but I wonder if you could ask Burton for a copy of Chuck's report."

"Whatever for?"

"I'd like to review it." Here he was again, throwing professional ethics to the wind.

"I don't see how I could do that, Andrew. Charlie might find out and think I was checking up on him."

"Well . . . it was just a thought."

"I wouldn't worry, Andrew. Dan has an excellent reputation. Charlie says he could be head of a department at some major medical center, but he prefers the rural life. I have no question about his competence. And I'm so relieved, I can't tell you. My only regret is that I didn't think of you sooner, and I spent all those years worrying unnecessarily."

"Hmm."

"Are you coming to the races next weekend? Chuck competes in the Singles. If he wins he goes to Henley."

"You bet. I wouldn't miss 'em."

"Come sit with us. We always do a picnic below the grandstand. And be sure to pray for good weather. I'll be a nervous wreck, of course. And as for Charlie—I don't know what I'll do with him. I just hope he doesn't drink too much."

"I'll see you Saturday," Fenimore said.

As soon as he hung up, he reached for a thick volume in the bookcase. The *AMA Directory of Physicians.* He flicked through the *B*s: Barton, Burcell, Burton, Daniel. Cardiologist. Board Certified. Chief of Cardiology, Pine Lake Hospital, Pine Lake, Pennsylvania. He called information for the doctor's number, then dialed it. As the phone rang, Fenimore realized it was after five and he would probably get a recorded message.

"Dr. Burton's office," a perky female voice with a slight upstate accent answered.

They still hold evening office hours in Pine Lake? Maybe I should move there. "This is Andrew Fenimore from Philadelphia. I'd like to make an appointment with Dr. Burton for a cardiac evaluation."

"From Philadelphia?" To upstate people, Philadelphia is the home of the devil. "Who referred you?"

Fenimore knew she was trying to figure out why anyone from a city with umpteen famous hospitals and thousands of specialists would come to Pine Lake for a medical exam. Good question. "I'm a cardiologist myself and heard about Dr. Burton through the grapevine. He has an excellent reputation."

"I see." Light dawned. A doctor from the big city wants to keep his medical history private so he chooses a doctor from out of town. "Let me check our calendar."

While Fenimore waited, he wondered at his own audacity. He wasn't exactly heeding Charlie's warning.

"Yes, Doctor. We could fit you in this Friday—at two o'clock."

Fenimore was amazed that the old professional courtesies were still intact at Pine Lake; the receptionist was obviously doing him a special favor.

"That should give you plenty of time to drive up here and back the same day," she went on. "But, if you want to stay overnight, there's a nice B & B down the road. Pine Haven. I could give you their number."

"Thanks. That's very kind." He jotted down the number. He didn't particularly want to stay overnight, but you never know what delays you may run into, and it might be a good idea to have a Plan B, he decided. Maybe Jennifer would like to come along. He called Pine Haven and made a reservation for a double room.

CHAPTER 9

The rest of the week went by in a whirl. Fenimore was too busy to get down to the river again, and Mrs. Doyle was swamped with paperwork. One evening his nurse stayed so late, Fenimore asked why she was still there.

"Well, I'm doing the work of two, you know," she grumbled.

"Of course." He caught her meaning. "Tell you what, I'll pick up Rat after school tomorrow and bring him here. He's probably bored silly sitting home every afternoon in front of the boob tube."

"That's a good idea, Doctor. He watches far too much TV anyway."

Fenimore smiled, knowing that Mrs. Doyle's TV was on nonstop when she was at home. "I'll take care of it. Now skedaddle! This stuff can wait 'til tomorrow." He shoved her purse at her and pointed her to the door.

When Fenimore called Rat to suggest his idea, Mrs. Lopez answered the phone.

"How's the patient?" Fenimore asked.

"Oh, Doctor, I'm so glad you called. I'm worried about him."

"His ankle?" Fenimore was alarmed.

40

"No. But I've noticed he's been eating more than usual."

"That's hardly a cause for concern." Fenimore chuckled. "He's a growing teenager."

"But he's not getting any exercise. Why would he need to eat so much? Sometimes he puts away a gallon of milk a day, and once he ate a whole loaf of bread between breakfast and lunch."

"It's probably boredom. Which brings me to the reason I called. Mrs. Doyle is missing his services at the office. Would it be all right if I taxied him to and from work after school until his ankle has healed?"

"Oh, Doctor, that's a wonderful idea, because that's the other thing I was worried about. He's been coming home late from school. Sometimes he's not home until four or five o'clock, and I don't know what he's up to."

Mrs. Lopez worked full-time and always worried about the threat of drugs and gangs in the neighborhood. She tried to keep an eye on her son, but it wasn't easy.

"Have you asked him what he's 'up to'?"

"Oh, I couldn't do that. Ray and I have a very trusting relationship."

Except, you don't trust him, Fenimore thought. "Well, once he gets back to work, all these problems will be solved."

"Oh, yes. I was so happy when he began working for you, Doctor. It kept him busy and out of trouble. And you're such a good influence—now that his father's gone."

"Well," Fenimore cleared his throat, "tell Rat . . . er . . . Ray, I'll pick him up outside the playground tomorrow at three o'clock sharp."

"Don't worry, he'll be there," Mrs. Lopez said with fervor.

"I'll be where?" Fenimore heard his young employee's querulous voice in the background. There must have been a commercial break and he had caught his mother's closing words.

On the way to pick up Horatio the next afternoon, Fenimore had an idea. He was anxious to discourage his protégé's interest in

41

skateboarding. He knew the statistics for injuries, and even for mortality, among the young. They were alarming. But the way to discourage him was not to forbid it. Everyone knew that was bad psychology. Instead you had to offer an alternative. And Fenimore had the perfect one. Rowing. Yes, that was it. He would introduce Rat to the joys of rowing, just as his father had introduced him. Fenimore felt a glow of pride at coming up with such a brilliant idea. His plan would have to wait until Rat recovered from his injury. But, at the first opportunity, he would take the boy down to the river. After one ride in a shell, he would never look at a skateboard again. Fenimore was whistling cheerfully as he pulled up to the school playground. Behind the chain-link fence, a couple of youths were tossing a basketball around, taking shots at a rusted rim with no basket. But no sign of Horatio.

Fenimore checked his watch. 3:10. He kept the motor running and turned on the radio. The dial was set to FM. He switched to AM to see if he could catch the Phillies game. They were playing the Mets today. Five to one. Phillies. He thought of his friend Rafferty. The police detective and the Phillies were like Siamese twins. You couldn't think of one without the other. He hadn't seen Raff for a while. He should give him a call.

A bunch of noisy boys and girls, horsing around, passed the car, but no Horatio. Where was that kid? Kept after school for some misdemeanor? Fenimore remembered a time when throwing spitballs was the worst offense you could commit in school. Today, they were lucky if they came home alive.

Then he saw him. A black ghost swinging around the corner on yellow crutches. He always wore black. Fenimore had never seen him wear anything else. Black T-shirt, black cargo pants, black sneakers. Even his accessories were black. Black backpack, black baseball cap, turned backward.

"Yo, Doc!" He deftly switched one crutch to his left hand, opened the car door with his right, shed his backpack, tossed his crutches into the backseat, and slipped into the passenger seat—all in, what seemed to Fenimore, one fluid motion. Not for the first time, Fenimore realized the boy was endowed with the grace of a natural athlete, and he began to entertain thoughts of turning him into a competitive rower. But not today. Plenty of time for that.

"Sorry I'm late. Had to see a friend."

Now there was an evasive explanation if ever there was one. Maybe Mrs. Lopez did have grounds for worry. "How's the ankle?"

"Good. Soon I'll be surfing again."

Fenimore let that go. He had the remedy, but all in good time. "Mrs. Doyle has really missed you," he said as he pulled out into Porter Street.

"Missed my filing, you mean."

"Well . . . that too."

"How is the old b—" He caught himself.

"Right as rain." Fenimore found Broad Street and joined the flow of traffic north, toward City Hall. During the ride, he became conscious of his companion's unusual silence. "Everything okay at school?" he asked.

"Uh-huh."

It wasn't Fenimore's style to force people to talk, but he decided to risk one more question. "Something bothering you?"

"No, man." Irritably.

Fenimore glanced at him. The boy was staring straight ahead, his mouth set in a grim line. Fenimore asked no more, but he felt uneasy. He resolved to keep an eye on him. When they reached Fenimore's house, the boy got out, retrieved his crutches and backpack, and swiftly mounted the marble steps. Mrs. Doyle must have been watching for him because she opened the door right away. She wore an uncharacteristic welcoming smile.

Fenimore went in search of a parking space.

CHAPTER 10

Fenimore found a spot for his car on the other side of Broad Street. But instead of going back to the office, he decided to drop by the police administration building to see his old friend Dan Rafferty. Besides wanting to catch up with the detective, he had a question for him.

"Well, look what the cat dragged in!" Rafferty raised his shaggy head from a daunting pile of paper and grinned at Fenimore.

The detective's office was shabby and stuffy, but he had a spectacular view of Independence Hall and the never-ending stream of antlike tourists prowling around outside. Rafferty had long ago ceased to notice his view, but his visitors were always awed by it.

This office with the view had been part of the lure the police department brass had used to get Rafferty off the street when he reached forty-five. The detective wasn't fooled by the view or the new title of "Inspector" they bestowed on him, but he knew his stamina and reflexes weren't what they used to be, and he had grudgingly acquiesced.

The only evidence of the detective's private life was a family photo, pushed to one side of his desk to make room for the mass of files that covered it. The photo was old. The cherubic tykes smiling from the frame were now sullen teenagers, and their mother, Mary, had put on a few pounds and acquired some gray hair.

"To what do I owe this rare pleasure?"

"Shut up, Raff. I know it's been awhile. But it looks like you haven't been exactly idle either." Fenimore waved at the cluttered desk.

Rafferty grunted. "Wish I were back on the street. Thought computers were supposed to get rid of paper. All they do is make more of it. . . ."

This familiar refrain had become a ritual with Rafferty. Fenimore had learned to let it run its course before trying to get his friend's attention. "How 'bout those Phils," Fenimore finally broke in.

"Yeah. Did you see them today? Beat the hell out of the Mets. Five to one."

"Yeah, I heard." Fenimore pulled a chair up to the desk and sat down.

"What's on your mind?" At last the detective had run out of complaints.

"Just a minor legal question."

Rafferty was instantly alert. He knew his friend's predilection for dabbling in detective work. He heartily disapproved, but found it interesting all the same.

"What would the penalty be for a doctor caught rifling through another doctor's case files? Not lifting anything, mind you. Just taking a peek."

Rafferty scratched his head. "Depends on the other doctor. If he brushes it off, you're home free. If he decides to press charges, you could be in deep trouble—a stiff fine, or even a prison sentence."

"Hmm. Not to mention what the AMA ethics committee would do to me . . . er . . . him," Fenimore grumbled.

"Mincemeat," Rafferty said. He looked at him quizzically. "What are you up to, Fenimore?"

"Just a little detective work." He told him about Chuck Ashburn.

"Isn't there some other way you could get a look at his file? Make up a story that you're doing a study on SCD in athletes, and you need data."

Fenimore thought about this and shook his head. "Wouldn't work. He'd be sure to tell Charlie and he'd know what I was up to."

"Well, I sure wouldn't risk my whole career on such a venture." Rafferty looked stern.

"How's the family?" Fenimore asked, to change the subject.

"Terrific. Dan Jr.'s flunking algebra. Molly's in love with a high school dropout. Mikey wants to be a racecar driver when he grows up. And Mary's sorry she didn't take the veil."

"Status quo."

"Right." He laughed. "I can't wait 'til *you* tie the knot. How's Jennifer?"

"Fine." Fenimore was amazed to find himself blushing.

"Still hangin' in there? Well, watch yourself, Doc. She won't stick around forever. How long you been goin' together?"

Fenimore shrugged. "Three or four years."

"See—you don't even know. Bad sign."

"I'd better get back to the office." Fenimore was anxious to end the conversation.

"Let's make a date at the Raven real soon," Rafferty said.

"You bet." Fenimore hurried away.

CHAPTER 11

Fenimore returned to his office and a placid scene: his nurse/office manager busily typing, with a cup of tea at her side; his office assistant busily filing, his iPod firmly attached to his ears; his cat sleeping peacefully on the windowsill, with her paws tucked under her chin. All was right with the world—except for that small nagging doubt Rafferty had planted in his mind about Jennifer. He entered his inner office and gave her a call.

"Nicholson's Books," her familiar voice answered.

"I'd like a copy of *Gone with the Wind* in Serbo-Croatian."

"Sorry. We just had a run on that and sold our last copy."

"Pshaw! And I wanted to give it to my mother-in-law for her birthday."

"Well, we have *Wuthering Heights* in Farsi."

"Oh no. She's afraid of heights."

"Then how about *Notes from the Underground* in Russian?"

"Hmm. Let me think about it."

Jennifer cut short the banter. "What's up?"

"Could you take a drive to the Poconos with me tomorrow?"

"What's in the Poconos?"

"Mountains, lakes, pine trees—"

"I mean, why are you going there?"

"For a physical checkup."

"What's wrong?" Her voice was sharp with anxiety.

Feeling guilty, but also gratified, he said, "Nothing. Just routine. But it would be nice to have company." He paused. "We could make a night of it. It should be pretty this time of year. I've got the name of a B & B," he said hopefully.

"Why not? I have a helper coming in tomorrow. Dad won't have to cover the shop alone. What time is your exam?"

"Two o'clock. I'll pick you up at eleven." He hung up before she could change her mind.

The ride to the Poconos was uneventful. Except for an occasional forsythia bush in bloom and the pale green haze in the treetops where budding leaves were beginning to show, spring was coyly hiding her charms. And the farther north they drove, the more bashful she became.

"We're about a week too early," Fenimore said.

"Oh no. I like early spring. I'll bet if we took a walk in the woods we'd see the skunk cabbage poking up."

He glanced at his companion in amazement. "What do you know about skunk cabbage? I thought you were a city girl."

"Not always. My grandfather had a farm in Lancaster County. He knew all about nature. When I was little he used to take me for long walks in the woods."

"Hmm. That's the first time I've heard of that."

"There are lots of things you haven't heard of."

He gave her a sidewise look. Had he detected a note of bitterness?

They rode in silence until Jennifer spied a sign. "Pine Lake. Five miles," she read.

Fenimore glanced at the clock on the dashboard. One thirty. They'd made good time. They had been climbing a winding, wooded road for several miles, and Fenimore's ears were popping. As they neared the crest, the road emerged from the woods into

48

an open space with a view of the mountains. A gentle haze encircled their blue caps.

"Nice," murmured Jennifer.

"Uh-huh." Fenimore reached for her hand and pressed it.

With a smile she returned the pressure.

Perhaps he *had* been taking her for granted lately. He would make up for it in the future. "I'm glad you came," he said.

Spring may have been hiding her face, but her scents were strong as they stepped out of the car. The air was pungent with the smell of growing things.

"The last thing I want to do is go see a doctor," Fenimore grumbled.

"As soon as you're done we'll go for a walk," Jennifer promised. "And I'll teach you about the birds and the flowers—"

"What about the bees?" He cast her a lascivious look.

"Come on." She grabbed his hand. "Let's get this over with."

CHAPTER 12

The receptionist did not look as perky as she had sounded. And she was older. About sixty. She ordered Fenimore to the back recesses of the office and told him to get undressed. Jennifer took a seat in the waiting room and tried to concentrate on an article on fly-fishing in *Field & Stream*.

While waiting for Dr. Burton to make his appearance, Fenimore, clad in only a hospital gown, shivered and tried to read *Time* with a picture of Saddam Hussein on the cover. Was there some secret medical code requiring outdated magazines and Arctic temperatures in examining rooms? If there was, he and Doyle didn't abide by it. Their examining room was toasty warm and their magazines were hot off the press (well, mostly). Another part of the code was to keep the patient waiting for at least twenty minutes so he could work up a good case of nerves and high blood pressure before seeing the doctor. After all, it would be such a waste if the doctor found nothing wrong with the patient.

Fenimore, although feeling fit as a fiddle when he arrived, now suffered from symptoms ranging from headache to shortness of breath to rapid heartbeat. Of course, this could be the onset of hypothermia. He glanced at his watch. Only five minutes had passed.

By the code, he still had fifteen minutes to go. Now would be a good time to snatch a peek at the Ashburn file. (Besides, it might be warmer in the file room. It was important to keep all those medical records comfortable.) He slid off the examining table and opened the door a crack. He had seen a nurse enter a room across the hall, carrying a pile of manila folders. After glancing up and down the hall, he padded barefoot to the door and tried the knob. It turned. He ducked inside. It *was* warmer here. Quite comfortable, in fact. His teeth even stopped chattering. He scanned the filing cabinets that lined the walls. All were labeled PATIENT FILES. Fortunately, the habit of computer filing had not reached this rural, upstate neighborhood. Each drawer was labeled alphabetically. The top drawer of the first cabinet read A–C. Cautiously, he pulled it out. Locating the Ashburn file easily, he was leafing through it when he heard footsteps in the hall.

"Dr. Fenimore?" The nurse was looking for him.

He had replaced the file and shut the drawer before the door opened. The nurse stared at him.

"Sorry," he mumbled, "I was looking for the bathroom."

The nurse's eyes narrowed. "At the other end of the hall, on your right," she said shortly.

As he slid past her, she added, "When you're finished, the doctor is waiting for you."

Let him wait, thought Fenimore, *and may he freeze his buns off!*

Once inside the bathroom, Fenimore leaned his head against the cool tile wall. He had worked up quite a sweat in the file room. But it had been worth it. He reviewed what he had learned. Chuck suffered from SCD, just like his father. Not only that, but he had *received a defibrillator implant at Pine Lake Hospital a year ago!*

Dr. Burton was nondescript. Middle-height, middle-weight, middle-aged. His face had no distinguishing features. Everything could have been store-bought from the same manufacturer—eyes, nose, mouth—and attached with machinelike precision. The label on the box—WHITE, MIDDLE CLASS, PROFESSIONAL, MALE. His manner was as familiar to Fenimore as an old pair of bedroom slippers. Patronizing, with a twist of bounce, and as much pizzazz as a goldfish.*

"Well, Doctor, what brings you to the boondocks from that sacred medical citadel—Philadelphia?" Burton asked.

"You come highly recommended," Fenimore said, smiling fatuously.

"By whom?"

"Uh . . . a friend." Fenimore rushed on. "I'm thinking of taking up rowing again and thought I'd better get my ticker checked out."

"I see." He examined the electrocardiogram his nurse had taken earlier and compared it to an older one Fenimore had brought with him. "Everything looks normal for someone your age," he said. "I don't see any reason why you shouldn't row, as long as it's just recreation."

"You can count on that. I'm not about to compete for the Diamond Sculls." Fenimore forced a laugh.

The doctor pressed his icy stethoscope against Fenimore's chest, then his back, listening intently. When he was finished, he said, "Actually, a friend of mine has a son who's trying for Henley. Maybe you know him. He was at Penn around your time. Charlie Ashburn?"

"The name's familiar," Fenimore mumbled.

"As for me, I don't go in for those old-fashioned sports," Burton said. "Give me a motor boat with plenty of horsepower."

"Um" was all Fenimore could muster as the doctor felt his groin and shot a finger up his rectum.

Removing his latex gloves, Dr. Burton tossed them into the nearby wastebasket and made a notation on Fenimore's chart. "Wouldn't hurt to have a colonoscopy," he said perfunctorily. "A good precaution at your age."

Fenimore nodded and immediately blocked on the suggestion. Like most doctors, he avoided medical examinations whenever

*Apologies to all goldfish advocates.

possible—unless he needed information for an investigation, such as now. He shivered on the examining table and eyed his clothes yearningly where they hung from a hook on the back of the door.

Burton continued, "I try to get down to the Mother Church for those Saturday afternoon lectures. When you live in the boonies it's important to make an effort to keep up," he added piously. ("Mother Church" was some alums' fond nickname for the Hospital of the University of Pennsylvania.)

Fenimore nodded, keeping his teeth tightly clenched to prevent their chattering.

"I think you're in good shape," Burton said at last. "I'll send you a report when the lab tests come back." He stuck out his hand.

"Thank you, Doctor," Fenimore shook the proffered hand fervently, thankful that the session had come to an end.

"By the way . . ."

Fenimore groaned inwardly.

". . . what was your frat at HUP?"

"AMPO," Fenimore uttered the name quickly, hoping to close the interview.

"No kidding?" He positively beamed at him. "We're brothers, then!"

For a moment Fenimore was afraid the doctor was going to hug him. Great. The last thing he wanted was for Burton to remember him, let alone with fraternal affection.

As soon as the door closed, Fenimore sprang from the examining table and donned his clothes with the zeal of an explorer returning from an Antarctic expedition. As he tied his shoes, he wondered about Charlie. Had he deliberately lied about Chuck's condition? Or had Dr. Burton lied to Charlie about his son's health? In either case, the question was—Why?

Fenimore appeared in the waiting room, fully clad, and reported his clean bill of health to Jennifer.

"Let's go for that walk," Jennifer said.

Despite his good news, Fenimore was subdued when they

reached the car. Once inside, he told Jennifer the real reason for his trip to the Poconos—and what he had discovered.

"I know you've told me how a defibrillator works, but could you refresh my memory?"

"When the heart muscle fibrillates, i.e. quivers and stops pumping blood, the defibrillator—or ICD—delivers an electric shock that stops the fibrillating and causes the heart to resume its normal rhythm. It also records the type of event and the time it occurred. The patient carries a special card that contains all the data needed to read the information from the ICD so the medic or doctor involved can figure out what happened. It's called an 'interrogation card.'"

"What does an ICD look like?"

"It's about the size of half a pack of cigarettes and fits under the skin of the chest, hardly visible to the naked eye."

"Is the operation risky?"

"Not at all. It's done on an outpatient basis and usually takes no more than a few minutes."

"But why did Chuck need one?"

"Because he suffers from SCD, just like his father."

"Then why is he rowing?"

"Because, apparently, Charlie is so keen on his son going to Henley, he's willing to risk the boy's life to send him there."

Jennifer shook her head, appalled. "What are you going to do?"

"The first thing is to get back to Philly and stop Chuck from racing tomorrow. This is the big race in which the two top singles rowers compete to go to Henley. Chuck will be competing against Hank Walsh."

"But how will you explain how you found out?"

"I'll worry about that after I stop him." He looked grim.

"So much for our idyllic mountain weekend," Jennifer said wistfully.

"I'm sorry," he said. "We'll come again," he promised, "when all this is over and spring has really sprung." He kissed her lightly on the cheek and turned the key in the ignition.

Nothing happened.

He tried again.

Dead.

"Oh my God. Did I leave my lights on?" He checked the knob. It was turned to "Off." He pulled the lever that opened the hood and leapt out. When he came back, he was shaking his head. "The battery looks all right, but I'll need a jump. I'll go inside and call a garage."

"Don't bother. I have my cell." She pulled it out. "Do you belong to AAA?"

He nodded, and dug the card from his wallet. When she called, they told her there would be a half-hour wait.

"We might as well take that walk," Fenimore said gloomily. They left the car and set off down the road.

CHAPTER 13

Sorry, folks. This isn't a simple jump job. You need a new alternator." The AAA man gave them the bad news. "I can tow you to the nearest garage. It's just down the road."

"But I have to get back to Philadelphia."

"If Virgil's not busy . . ."

Virgil?

". . . he can probably fix it for you by late afternoon," the man said.

Resigned, Fenimore shouted, "Tow away!" He and Jennifer climbed into the cab.

Virgil wasn't busy, but he was talkative, and he didn't seem in any hurry to fix the car. Fenimore and Jennifer quickly realized that as long as they hung around, the mechanic would talk more than work. They asked him to direct them to the nearest restaurant.

"There's a diner down the road on the left," he said in a disappointed tone, sorry to lose his audience.

"Down the road" turned out to be over a mile. Jennifer had worn sensible shoes, a pair of clogs, but Fenimore had on a pair of relatively new oxfords with slippery soles and his progress was slow. But it was a pretty walk. The birds were out in full force, building their nests for the coming broods. A row of forsythia bushes was in full bloom. And Jennifer actually spied a skunk cabbage poking its bright green snout through a patch of leftover snow.

The diner was vintage 1930s with no frills or phony additions. Over bowls of homemade vegetable soup and chunks of warm, freshly baked bread, Fenimore explained the medical implications of Chuck's condition to Jennifer.

"Sudden cardiac death is a gamble. You can lead a perfectly normal life with the tendency and never have it kick in—doing everything anyone else does—*except strenuous exercise*. Chuck could jog, swim, shoot baskets, even row—as long as he doesn't make excessive demands on his heart. Recreational sports would be relatively safe. It's the competitive sports that are dangerous!" He broke off a piece of bread and debated about adding butter.

"Oh, go ahead." Jennifer read his mind. "You're on vacation."

He frowned. "Some vacation."

"In small measure, life may perfect be," Jennifer quoted.

"Who said that?"

"Ben Jonson."

"Umph." But he spread a small amount of butter on the bread.

"You know," Jennifer mused, "sports aren't only about physical fitness."

"How's that?"

"Well, surely you know that sports build character."

"Like taking steroids?"

"I'm not talking about professional sports."

"What sports did you play?" he asked.

"Field hockey."

"What position?"

"Goalie."

"Goalie?" Fenimore sat back to better survey the petite woman before him. "I thought goalies had to be big enough to cover the goal."

"Wrong. They have to be alert and quick on their feet."

"But how does that build character?"

"There are times in life when we all have our backs to the wall and have to come out fighting."

Fenimore nodded. "True."

"Also, there are times in life when everything runs smoothly, but you shouldn't become complacent or a forward will come charging down the field and shoot a ball right between your legs." Jennifer was growing animated. Fenimore sensed she was reliving a game from long ago. He was sure she was smelling the newly cut grass, the sweat of her teammates, the tangy odor of orange slices that were served at the half. "Or," she went on, "even worse, a forward will pass the ball to a left inner or a right wing and, while you're looking the other way, they'll sneak the ball into the goal—behind you."

"Now that does sound like real life—at a medical center," Fenimore said. After ordering two coffees, he turned back to Jennifer. "Were you a good goalie?" he asked. Even if she were wrapped in thick pads and a mask, it was hard for him to imagine this slight woman defending a vast space with only her body and a thin stick.

"I was on the varsity team for four years," she said. "But I didn't bring this up to brag," she added hastily. "I just wanted to point out that you shouldn't belittle the role of sports in a kid's life. Academia is all very well, but learning how to hold your own on a ball field—or on a river—teaches important lessons too."

"Touché," Fenimore said, taking a sip of his coffee. "I would have loved to have seen you in action. Did your father come to your games?"

"Once."

"Only once?"

"It was the one game in which I was hit on the head by a ball. I was knocked out cold. He never came again." Jennifer laughed.

"Holy mackerel! You really got clobbered?"

"Yep. I told you, athletics is not all about physical fitness. That blow knocked some sense into my head."

"I hadn't noticed," Fenimore teased.

When they returned to the garage, Fenimore's car was still on the lift and Virgil was nowhere to be seen.

"Hell," Fenimore said. "Where could he be?"

"Virgil!" Jennifer sang into the dark garage.

No answer.

They wandered around to the back, where they found the missing mechanic. He was seated at a battered picnic table enjoying a late lunch washed down with a Budweiser.

"Oh my God," muttered Fenimore.

"Are you almost finished?" asked Jennifer.

"Just one more bite." He held up the remains of a squashed cupcake.

"I meant with our car."

"Oh." He ran a hand through his patchy hair and studied the remains of his lunch. "I have bad news. There's this missing part. I sent my son to town for it, but I close at four and—"

"Look," Fenimore broke in desperately, "I'll pay you extra if you'll finish the job tonight."

"Gee, that's real nice." Virgil grinned. "But it's the wife's birthday and I promised to take her out to dinner."

So, when Virgil's son came back (Ajax was his name), he drove Fenimore and Jennifer in his pickup back to the Pine Haven B & B. They spent a restless, unromantic night among a million gewgaws and two Pekinese dogs, who took turns yapping at their door until dawn.

CHAPTER 14

When Fenimore called the next morning, Virgil said, "The car won't be ready until noon." To keep Fenimore from blowing a gasket, Jennifer led him on a walk through a wooded glen behind the B & B. She tried to teach him how to identify trees by their bark, the difference between fox and dog tracks, and the mating habits of certain birds.

"What about the bees?" Fenimore repeated his earlier complaint.

"It's too early for them. We have to come back in June," she said.

"Over my dead body," he seethed.

Once on the road, Jennifer had to caution Fenimore frequently about the speed limit. He knew the big Singles race between Chuck and Hank Walsh was in the afternoon, but he didn't know the exact time. As he sped down the Pennsylvania Turnpike he kept an anxious eye on the dashboard clock. Since it was Saturday, Jennifer suggested they listen to the Metropolitan Opera broadcast. "They're doing *Don Giovanni* today," she said. "Your favorite." But when she turned it on, the high-pitched arias even got on her nerves and she snapped it off. Anxiety and opera don't mix, she decided.

When they reached the Schuylkill Expressway they hit a traffic jam. Jennifer was afraid Fenimore was going to have a stroke. "Want me to drive for a while?" she offered, out of self-preservation more than kindness.

"No," he snapped.

"They're probably going to the regatta too," she said.

"They should stay home and read a book," Fenimore said unreasonably.

Meanwhile, at Fenimore's office, Mrs. Doyle was working away, still playing catch-up for all the days her assistant had been home nursing his broken ankle. She was just finishing up when the phone rang. A phone call on Saturday afternoon was unusual. Mrs. Doyle lifted the receiver. It was Mrs. Lopez—and she sounded upset.

"What time did Ray leave?" she asked.

"The usual time—about 12:01," Mrs. Doyle told her.

"Well, he's not home yet. Do you know where he could be?"

Mrs. Doyle tried to remember if Horatio had mentioned anything about going someplace after work. His conversations with the nurse were usually monosyllabic, and she couldn't remember him saying anything to her but "Hi" and "So long." "I can't think of a thing," said Mrs. Doyle. "I ordered a cab for him, gave him some money out of petty cash, and thought he was going straight home."

The silence at the other end of the line quivered with anxiety.

"Could he have stopped off at a friend's house?" Mrs. Doyle suggested. "Or gone to a music store?" She knew how Rat loved his CDs.

"He wouldn't have given up the cab too far from home," his mother said. "He can't walk more than a few blocks with those crutches."

Mrs. Doyle considered. "I could call the cab company. They keep records of all their passenger pickup and drop-off locations," she offered.

"Oh, would you, Mrs. Doyle? I'd be so—"

Doyle heard a door slam in the background over Mrs. Lopez's voice.

"*There you are!* Where have you been?"

Mrs. Doyle gently replaced the receiver.

Gradually the traffic loosened up and Fenimore was able to escape the expressway via the ramp near the zoo. He maneuvered his way through the narrow streets of Brewery Town, past the golden statue of Joan of Arc, to Eakins Circle, below the art museum. Kelly Drive was cordoned off by yellow police tape for the regatta and every parking space was taken.

"Pull over and get out," Jennifer said. "I'll park the car and meet you later."

Fenimore obeyed. As he jumped out he called back, "Come to the picnic ground below the grandstand. I'll be with the Ashburn party."

The last Jennifer saw of him, he was making his way up the parkway toward Kelly Drive, head down, his expression anxious. In his business suit, regimental striped tie, and oxfords, he stood out like a sore thumb among the rest of the crowd who were dressed for a casual Saturday afternoon in shorts and jeans, T-shirts and sweats. As he trudged off in the shadow of that great Greek monument, the Philadelphia Art Museum, dressed in the wrong clothes, to try to save a young man's life, Jennifer found his figure touching. It wasn't until she lost sight of him in the crowd that she moved on to look for a parking space.

CHAPTER 15

As Fenimore approached the grandstand, he paused to watch a race of eights finishing on the river. The contrast between the shells skimming effortlessly over the water and the extreme effort marking the faces of the eight men inside was almost comical. Once over the line, they slowed their pace, but did not stop until they had gone a dozen lengths. Then they collapsed, as if picked off by some hidden sniper. A few minutes later, however, they had recovered and were rowing toward the judges' stand to pick up their award. Fenimore moved swiftly on, berating himself for pausing for even a minute in his search for Chuck.

He saw Caroline first. Pale and strained, she was distributing sandwiches to a circle of friends seated on lawn chairs and blankets. Charlie, a paper cup in one hand and a pitcher of something pink in the other, was staggering among his guests, already seriously inebriated. There was a law against alcohol in Fairmount Park, and if caught with it, you paid a stiff fine. Although the stuff in Charlie's pitcher resembled lemonade, Fenimore was sure it was 90 percent vodka.

Caroline spied Fenimore and smiled, waving him over. Charlie caught sight of him at the same time and ostentatiously turned his back. He still had not forgiven Fenimore for meddling in his son's medical affairs.

"Can I speak to you for a moment?" Fenimore said to Caroline, keeping his voice low.

Alarmed by his grave expression, she nodded and they moved away from the party, to a cluster of trees.

"What's wrong, Andrew?"

He told her.

She turned a shade paler and leaned against the nearest tree for support.

"When is the Singles race?" he asked her.

"It's the next race." She glanced at her watch. "About twenty minutes."

"Where is Chuck?"

"I don't know." She shook her head. "At the boathouse . . . or upriver with O'Brien."

"We have to find him. I'll check the boathouse. You look for O'Brien."

They set off in opposite directions. Approaching the Windsor Club from the riverbank, Fenimore's oxfords echoed hollowly on the wooden dock. The boathouse was silent and deserted. The bays were empty. All the shells were either on the river or resting in slings on the riverbank. An uneasy feeling overcame Fenimore, as if the ghosts of all the young rowers—winners and losers— since 1860 were hovering there, waiting expectantly, like himself, for the big race to begin. This mood was broken by the sound of very unghostlike footsteps, on the dock. Fenimore looked up to see Hank Walsh coming toward him.

"Doctor? What brings you here?" He appeared relaxed and calm, despite the impending race.

"I'm looking for Chuck."

"He's not here. He usually sticks to himself before a race. You might find him upriver, near the starting line."

"Thanks—and good luck," he added.

Hank nodded and went to collect his shell from its sling.

Fenimore hastened back to the picnic ground, scanning the crowd for Caroline or O'Brien. Caroline saw Fenimore first and came rushing up. "O'Brien and the boys are at the falls, where the race begins. I've asked a park groundskeeper to drive you up there in his cart." She led Fenimore to the keeper.

"Hop on," the man said cheerfully. "These things move faster than you think. And I have a horn!" He beeped it twice.

Fenimore climbed in.

"We're off!" said the keeper, giving a sharp beep that sent the cluster of people in front of him scattering.

Fenimore sat forward, peering ahead, hoping for a glimpse of Chuck.

CHAPTER 16

As the cart scooted through the crowd, scattering people in its wake, Fenimore tried to think what he was going to say to Chuck. He had nothing in mind other than, "Stop, you damned fool! Do you want to kill yourself?" Hardly the best approach. Within a few minutes, he caught sight of the Falls Bridge and the starting line, designated by a row of colorful buoys. "You can let me out here," he told the driver.

"If you need a lift back, just give a whistle," the driver said with a wink.

"Thanks." Fenimore was already scanning the riverfront for Chuck. He spotted O'Brien, squatting under a tree, surrounded by a group of young rowers. He appeared to be giving them a postrace pep talk. Fenimore hated to interrupt, but this was a matter of life and death. "Excuse me, I'm looking for Chuck," he said.

O'Brien glanced at his watch. "He likes to keep to himself before a race," he said, with a frown. "Can't it wait 'til later?"

"I'm afraid not." *Definitely not*, thought Fenimore. He debated whether to tell O'Brien about his discovery. He decided against it. This was Chuck's decision; no one could make it for him.

"Well, you may find him down there." The coach gestured at the riverbank

Fenimore had gone only a few yards when he saw Chuck. He was sitting on the bank, his back to Fenimore. Fenimore recognized the boy by the number six on his shirt, and by his shell—*The Zephyr*—that was tied to the wharf below him. He seemed to be in deep contemplation. Fenimore wondered if he practiced yoga. So many young people did today. Not a bad way to get your nerves in order. He even recommended it to some of his patients. He hated to disturb him, but— "Chuck!"

The boy looked around.

"Could I speak to you for a minute?"

"It's almost race time." Polite, but resolute.

"It's very important. I've talked to Dr. Burton. . . ."

Chuck came alive. He scrambled down to the wharf, grabbed his oars, and settled into his shell.

"Wait!" Fenimore scurried down the bank, slipping and sliding in his oxfords.

Chuck dipped his oars and pulled swiftly away from the dock.

Fenimore looked after him and his heart sank like one of those leaden stones by the river's edge. Turning his back on the river, he went in search of the groundskeeper to cadge a ride to the grandstand. All he could do now was watch the race—and its finish.

When he arrived at the finish line, the race was just about to begin. The Ashburn party had deserted their picnic site and moved down to the water's edge to gain a better view. Fenimore hurried to join them. Caroline saw him, but there was no way she could leave Charlie at such a crucial moment. Fenimore shook his head, to let her know he had failed. Slowly she turned back to the river. Fenimore followed her gaze. The two singles shells were mere flyspecks on the water. It was impossible to tell which one was in the lead. He scanned the bank for the Walshes, to no avail. They would be easy to spot. There were next to no African Americans in this crowd. Rowing was still primarily a white sport, the way basketball was a black one. But this was changing. He had read somewhere that public high schools were introducing rowing into their curriculum and he had noticed shells for rent—to the public—near the Water Works.

The attention of the crowd was frozen on the rowers—two dark specks upriver. Fenimore could just make out the numbers on their shirts: Chuck's six and Hank's twenty-two. That was the frustrating thing about regattas. You couldn't watch the whole race at once. You could watch the beginning, the middle, or the end, depending on where you were situated. Most people opted for the excitement of the finish line.

As the two shells sped closer the crowd grew quieter. But as they drew abreast, and were neck and neck, a sound rose from the riverbank like the roar of a cataract. Fenimore stared intently at number six. Chuck's face was distorted beyond recognition by the enormity of his effort. Fenimore closed his eyes and prayed. Not for the boy's victory. For his survival.

An eerie hush fell. They must be nearing the finish line. Fenimore opened his eyes in time to see Chuck spurt over the line—a fraction of a second ahead of Hank.

He glanced to his left, where the Ashburns were standing. Charlie, red-faced, was screaming, stamping, and pounding his fist into his palm. Caroline, white and stiff, seemed to be still holding her breath. Friends of the Ashburns began crowding around them. The women squealing, the men alternately pumping Charlie's hand and pounding him on the back. Fenimore's gaze switched back to the oarsmen. They had continued to row a few lengths, lessening their pace gradually, as they had been taught. Then they raised their oars from the water, drifted to a halt, and slumped in their seats.

Hank recovered first. Fenimore saw him lift his hand and make a *V* sign to Chuck. Fenimore held his breath, until he saw Chuck slowly raise his hand in acknowledgment.

"Andrew!" Caroline had extricated herself from her ebullient guests and was making her way toward him. Her first words to him were, "He'll go to Henley now."

Fenimore nodded. "Congratulations," he murmured.

She stood, irresolute, confused. "You tried to stop him?"

"He wouldn't listen."

Charlie came up to recapture his wife. Ignoring Fenimore, he thrust a glass of champagne (disguised with a dash of orange juice) into her hand and pulled her back into the mêlée.

Fenimore saw the Walshes arrive and congratulate the Ashburns. Mrs. Walsh was a tiny birdlike woman. He wondered why she had been absent the night of the Ashburn dinner party. Maybe she didn't like such gatherings. Charlie was urging them to stay, trying to force glasses of champagne on them. They graciously refused and went away.

As Jennifer edged through the crowd, searching for Fenimore, an enormous cheer erupted near the river's edge. She craned her neck to see who had won. It was impossible to tell. She asked a pert coed who was jumping up and down nearby.

"Number six!" she cried gleefully.

"But who's number six?" Jennifer asked.

The girl looked at her in amazement. "Chuck, of course. Chuck Ashburn."

"Thanks." Jennifer's emotions took a roller-coaster ride. *Down.* Andrew had failed to stop Chuck from racing. *Up.* Chuck had won the race and survived!

She suddenly felt very tired. Those yapping dogs had kept her awake all night, then the tension of wondering if the mechanic would finish the car in time, followed by the hair-raising drive from Pine Lake to Philadelphia, and now the news that Chuck had won—and survived! She sat down on the grass to rest. She needed a breather, she decided, before facing the Ashburns and their obnoxious guests. Fleetingly, she wondered how the Walshes were feeling.

She tried to block out the noise of the crowd and focus on the serene flow of the river, the way her yoga teacher had taught her. But it was hard to concentrate in the midst of the excited youthful throng. They flowed around her, trying to avoid stepping on her hands and tripping over her feet. She stood up. On the whole, it was an orderly crowd. There was no sign of alcohol. Orange juice was the favored drink of the day. The bike path was lined with vendors selling bottled water and juice, plus T-shirts, caps, and programs. Jennifer was deciding whether to buy some juice when her attention was caught by male voices behind her. She didn't mean to eavesdrop, but . . .

"What are the chances of getting rid of those boathouses?" His voice was faintly familiar.

"Not good," came the answer.

"I have an idea."

"I'm listening."

"What if one of those rowers should have an accident?"

Newborn. Jennifer identified the first speaker—the developer at the Ashburn party.

They must have moved on because she couldn't hear his companion's answer. She cautiously turned. Neither man was in sight. Forgetting about the orange juice, Jennifer continued her search for Fenimore.

CHAPTER 17

Fenimore would have dearly liked to leave the Ashburn party. But he had to wait for Jennifer. Where could she be? He scanned the celebratory group for a friendly face. There were none. He stood uncomfortably on the sidelines until a lively voice, vaguely familiar, spoke to him from behind. "Why, I do believe it's Dr. Fenimore."

Turning, he saw an elderly woman in an elegant black pantsuit, enhanced by colorful costume jewelry, leaning on a cane. Without a doubt, she and Fenimore were the two best-dressed people on the Schuylkill that day.

"Mrs. Henderson!"

"Myra." She eyed him with a bemused expression.

"How are you? I haven't seen you since . . ." The last time he had seen her was at the funeral of a young woman.

"Let's not think about that," she said hastily. "Today is a day of celebration!"

"You're a friend of the Ashburns?"

"Oh yes. For many years. Charlie's mother and I were at school together. Now tell me what you've been up to. I see your name in the paper from time to time."

"Let me find you a chair." He spied a vacant lawn chair and dragged it over to his newfound friend.

She accepted the seat and gave him a keen look. "You aren't investigating any crimes today, I hope."

"Good grief, no," he said, a little too quickly. "I'm taking the day off."

"Hmm." She looked at him thoughtfully. Fenimore had forgotten how sharp she was.

"I'm waiting for a friend. You remember Jennifer?"

"Certainly. I would have thought you'd be married by now."

Fenimore blushed. Why was everyone so anxious to marry him off? First Rafferty, now Mrs. Henderson.

"How is that young man who saved your life?" she asked.

"Horatio?"

"Such an unusual name."

"Fine. Well, actually he's not fine. He broke his ankle skateboarding."

"Does he still work for you?"

He nodded. "After school and Saturday mornings."

"I thought he might go into medicine someday," she mused.

"Did you?" Fenimore was interested, because the same possibility had crossed his mind.

"I have a knack for ferreting out doctors," she said. "Remember how I discovered you?"

He certainly did. Mrs. Henderson had been in the hospital recovering from hip surgery when Fenimore had passed her room. She had called out, "Doctor!" And he had helped her get some medicine to relieve her pain.

"Have you recovered?" Fenimore asked, eyeing her cane.

"Oh yes. This thing is just for show." She gave the cane a shake. "In a crowd, if you carry a cane, they give you a little more room. Not always, but this is a pretty nice group."

"Have you been following Chuck's rowing career?" Fenimore asked.

"Oh yes. Charles has had that poor boy in a boat since he was a toddler. I've never approved of saddling kids with the thwarted ambitions of their parents. But no one listens to me since I never had any. Kids, that is, not ambitions," she amended quickly.

Fenimore smiled.

"I love the regattas and the old boathouses. I come down every spring. But Boathouse Row is at risk, you know." Her expression turned grave.

"Because of the marina, you mean?" He shook his head. "But Charlie is fighting it."

"So am I." She raised her chin and her look of determination would have daunted more than a city planner, Fenimore thought—say a Marine battalion?

"I'm president of the Pennsylvania Historical Society and we're working to get Boathouse Row certified as a historic landmark. If we succeed, no one will be able to touch it."

"Wonderful!" Fenimore felt good for the first time that day. "And what are your chances of success?"

"Excellent. Time is our only problem. The commission is trying to get their plan for the marina accepted before the certification goes through. If they succeed . . ." she left her sentence hanging. Her gaze had fixed on the pitcher of pink fluid that Charlie was offering his guests. "What in God's name is that?" she asked.

"Vodka disguised as pink lemonade, I think," said Fenimore.

"Yuck!"

The slang word uttered by such a distinguished lady tickled Fenimore.

"Charlie promised to bring me some martinis, but I guess he forgot."

"Can I get you something to drink?"

"No, thanks. I'd rather stay sober than let a drop of that pink poison down my throat." She reached into her petit-point bag and drew out a lighter and a cigarillo. There was a slight breeze and she had trouble lighting it. Fenimore helped her. Several Ashburn guests sent disapproving glances her way. Fenimore suspected this was exactly what the elderly woman desired. Although he smoked a pipe occasionally, Fenimore only did so in the privacy of his home.

"Where's your pipe?" asked Myra, a mischievous glint in her eye.

"At home in a drawer."

She frowned.

"Don't worry, I haven't given it up," he quickly assured her.

"Good." She nodded. "It's the minor vices that keep us from succumbing to the major sins."

Fenimore wondered if she was speaking from experience. "I expect you're right."

"Myra, dear . . ." An acquaintance charged up. Ignoring Fenimore, she directed her conversation exclusively to Mrs. Henderson.

Fenimore wandered off, feeling infinitely better about the chances of preserving Boathouse Row. Now where was Jennifer?

Jennifer spotted Fenimore first. She maneuvered her way through the crowd toward him. Catching his eye, she waved. As he hurried over, she asked, "Did you find Chuck?"

He nodded.

"What happened?"

"He refused to listen. He took off in his shell. There was nothing I could do."

"But he made it."

"Yes, he made it. *This* time," he added somberly.

Jennifer told him about the conversation she had overheard.

"An accident? Are you sure you heard right?"

Jennifer was sure.

As soon as one worry disappears, it is replaced by another. "It's a great life, if you don't weaken," he muttered.

"What?"

"An old saying of my grandmother's." He had never understood what it meant when he was a boy. Now he did.

74

CHAPTER 18

Over dinner at their favorite restaurant, the Silk City Diner, Fenimore was preoccupied. He toyed with his food, and all Jennifer's attempts at conversation fell flat. While waiting for their coffee, he blurted, "I can't believe that kid is going to row at Henley with a defibrillator!"

"Can't you stop him?" asked Jennifer.

"You saw how effective I was at stopping him today." He shook his head. "Basically, the responsibility for our health is up to us. It's a free country. All the authority of a major medical center can't force a patient to accept medical treatment or to stay within its walls. All a doctor can do is inform them of the benefits of taking his advice, and the consequences of refusing it. The patient can take it or leave it." He drained his coffee. "Remember Sweet Grass?" Fenimore was referring to a young woman who had refused medical treatment because it would have interfered with her wedding plans.

Jennifer nodded. "It's strange, isn't it, that we can be fined for not wearing a seat belt, but are free to refuse medical treatment that could save our life."

"All a physician can do is present the evidence in as convincing a manner as possible."

"And—have you done that?"

Fenimore looked at her sharply. "No, not really. All I did was shout that I had talked to Dr. Burton. There was no time for anything else."

"Maybe you should."

"You're damned right." He signaled the waitress for the check.

The next morning, Fenimore called Caroline and told her about his plan to speak to Chuck. He asked her if she would help him arrange a meeting. To his surprise, he found her uncooperative. It seemed she was no longer opposed to Chuck rowing at Henley. "After all, he survived yesterday's race with no ill effects," she said, "and he has a whole month to get back in shape for Henley."

Fenimore was speechless.

"It's quite a pageant, Andrew," she went on. "Everyone who's anyone in the rowing world will be there. They have cocktail parties, banquets, and high teas. The British always do everything so elegantly. All my friends are green with envy."

Fenimore stared at the receiver, unable to believe what he was hearing.

"I'm going to have to buy a whole new wardrobe." She laughed. "The Brits are a little more formal than we Philadelphians."

"But what about the risk?" Fenimore finally sputtered. "Nothing has changed. Chuck still suffers from SCD." He knew he was speaking too loudly.

"Really, Andrew, you do take the fun out of everything. This is a wonderful opportunity for Chuck. Indeed, for the whole family. It would be a tragedy for him to miss it. I have to run now. Bloomies is having a sale on evening wear. I can't miss it."

Fenimore continued holding the receiver until the operator began haranguing him: "Please hang up. Beep. Please hang up. Beep."

Mrs. Doyle stuck her head in the door. "Are you ready for your first patient?"

"Send them in," he said in a resigned voice.

· · ·

When morning office hours were over, Fenimore had an idea. He called Frank O'Brien.

"Sorry, Doc. My hands are tied. I'd like to stop the boy, but he's twenty-one. I can't force him to give up such an opportunity."

"But if it's a matter of life and death!"

"We don't know that, do we, Doctor? He survived yesterday's race. And he seemed as fit as ever at this morning's practice."

"But the odds—"

"I'm sorry. I really am." The coach hung up.

Damn. Now it was up to him to prevent Chuck from rowing at Henley. He would have to waylay him somehow and present his case. And it would have to be a good case. He would not have more than one chance and he didn't want to muff it.

CHAPTER 19

Fenimore continued his routine, which now included picking up Horatio every day after school and driving him to the office. One day, while he was waiting in his car for the boy, he saw a headline in *The Inquirer:*

Boathouse Row Due for Face-Lift

Famous Boathouse Row along the Schuylkill may soon be replaced by a more modern marina. Cornelius Wormwood, director of the City Planning Commission, announced the news today. By a narrow margin, the commission voted to include the site in their plan for redevelopment of the riverfront. A public hearing will be scheduled for those opposed in the near future.

Fenimore shoved the newspaper aside and glanced at the dashboard clock. 3:15. Where was that kid? Another ten minutes passed before Fenimore left his car (carefully locking it) and went to look for the boy. He didn't have to go far. A block from the school he spied a pair of crutches leaning against a brick wall. Next to them was the entrance to a cellar, its doors wide open. Peering down into the dark hole, he called, "Rat!"

No answer.

A ladder led from the sidewalk down to the cellar. Cautiously, Fenimore descended. The space below was dark, but enough light seeped in from the open door for him to see the room was full of trash. The smell of decaying garbage and excrement engulfed him, and he heard the patter of little feet—not the human kind. Reemerging into daylight, he returned to his car to find Rat (the human kind) leaning against the hood.

"Yo, Doc." He waved nonchalantly.

"Where the hell have you been?" Fenimore read him the riot act for keeping him waiting.

Horatio's cool evaporated and, to Fenimore's horror, his eyes filled with tears.

"Sorry," Fenimore hastily apologized. "I was worried about you. What were your crutches doing next to that cellar door?"

As soon as they were in the car, Horatio broke down. "There's this girl," he croaked. "She's homeless. And I'm sorta looking after her."

Fenimore listened attentively.

"I came on her one day after school. She was rooting through the trash. You know how they do."

Fenimore nodded.

"I didn't think nothing of it . . . until she looked up at me."

Fenimore waited.

"Her eyes were so sad. I had to do something."

Fenimore nodded again.

"I bought her a hot dog and a soda. She gulped it down like she'd never eaten before. After that, I brought her something every day."

"So that's where the food went."

Horatio looked up.

"Your mother's been worried about you, because you were eating so much."

He grinned, briefly, then went on in a rapid monotone. "She's thirteen. Her father's been hittin' up on her since she was ten. She told her mom, but her mom didn't do nothing. So she ran away."

Fenimore stared.

"Her name's Tanya," Horatio said.

Back home, Fenimore shut himself in his inner office to think. Horatio's story had shaken him. He knew such things went on. How could you not know? The media was full of it. But to actually know someone. Or rather, know someone who knew someone . . . Had things like this always gone on? But in the "good old days" they were closely kept family secrets. He had to help. He reached for the phone and punched in Rafferty's number.

"Long time no hear!" his friend said as soon as he heard Fenimore's voice.

"You never call me, either," Fenimore replied, thinking he sounded like a peevish, neglected girlfriend. "I have a problem."

"Don't we all."

"What's yours?" Fenimore was concerned.

"I was speaking generically. Let's have it."

Fenimore told him about Tanya.

"Where do you find these people, Fenimore?"

"This cellar door was open, and . . ."

"My God, didn't your mother ever tell you not to enter a house before you're asked? It's not polite."

"This was an abandoned house."

"So that makes it all right?"

Fenimore didn't answer. He was anxious to end the banter so the detective would give his problem serious thought.

"Normally, you should report a case like this to the Department of Human Services," he said slowly. "They would try to find a relative to take the girl until the investigation into child abuse is completed. If no relative is available, the girl would be assigned to a foster home."

"You said 'normally.' What about abnormally?"

"If I keep my mouth shut and you don't report the case, you could house her temporarily at your place. But you'd better have female chaperones around the clock—"

"In case I have a sudden urge to attack her?"

"Exactly."

"Weekdays would be no problem. Mrs. Doyle is here from nine to five every day. And, I guess I could ask Jennifer to come at night, and on the weekends."

"Great idea!" Rafferty chortled.

Ignoring him, Fenimore went on, thinking aloud. "Maybe Mrs. Lopez, Horatio's mother, could fill in for Jen, if Jen has something else to do."

"Well, you work it out," Rafferty said, "and let me know how things go."

"Right. Thanks, Raff."

"No problem. Mr. Fix-it, always at your service."

Even though the solution they had arrived at was only temporary, Fenimore felt relieved.

CHAPTER 20

Although occupied with the arrangements for Tanya's care, not to mention his medical practice, Fenimore did not forget Chuck. He combed all the recent medical journals for articles on SCD and ICD implants, and consulted a number of his colleagues on the subject to make sure he hadn't missed some new development in the field. In the end, he was forced to accept the unavoidable conclusion: No one with Chuck's condition should participate in competitive sports. Period. In other countries, such as Italy and Japan, the government took care of such matters. Every athlete was screened before they were allowed to take part in a sport. If they had a condition such as Chuck's, they were automatically eliminated from playing by law. Unfortunately, no such law existed in the United States.

After a brief tussle with his conscience, there was no doubt in Fenimore's mind as to what he should do. He knew he must confront Chuck, one-on-one, face-to-face, and try to convince him to give up the Henley race.

He knew Chuck's practice schedule—five to seven in the morning, and four to six in the afternoon. Caroline had told him.

He decided to waylay his prey in the morning, because he would be less likely to run into Charlie.

Dressed as if going for a row himself, Fenimore set out in his car at six thirty. He planned to arrive at the club after Chuck had showered. He would wait near the entrance and catch him as he was leaving. It was a fine spring morning and Fenimore wished he *were* going for a row, instead of facing such a painful encounter.

He passed the Lincoln statue on his right and turned into Sedgely Drive. The road was lined with cherry trees—"dressed in white for Eastertide" as Housman so aptly put it. Fenimore preferred to forget the rest of the poem; it dealt with the brevity of life, and depressed him.

There was no parking problem at this hour. He took out the thermos of Gatorade and two plastic cups that he had carefully prepared and laid them on the seat. Then he crossed Kelly Drive to the boathouse. Traffic was still a mere trickle. He passed a few young rowers, who cast him curious glances. *I guess they're wondering what Methuselah is doing up so early,* thought Fenimore. He stopped one of them: "Have you seen Chuck Ashburn?"

The youth glanced at his watch. "He's probably still out. He should be back in about twenty minutes."

Twenty minutes? Fenimore shivered. He wouldn't mind the chill if he were rowing, but standing around on the dock in a T-shirt and shorts was another matter. He went inside and was delighted to find a coffeepot and some cups set out on a table. He helped himself. Young men and women came and went around him. None of them seemed interested in either the coffee or him. They had other things on their minds, such as their fitness schedules and the next race. Fenimore sipped the warm brew and planned what he was going to say to Chuck.

Ultimately, as he had told Jennifer, the responsibility for people's lives rests in their own hands. We are as free to risk our lives as to preserve them. People do so every day. Parachuting, bungee jumping, riding motorcycles and racecars, mountain climbing and spelunking. Some people feel that living on the brink adds zest to life. How was Chuck's situation any different from theirs?

Yet it was.

But did Fenimore have any right to interfere? Not really. All he could do was present a strong argument for living a full life—having a career, marriage, a family, travel, retirement, hobbies. . . . He caught sight of Chuck at the bottom of the stairs. Chuck saw him at the same moment, and was about to dart up the stairs to the shower room. But Fenimore was too quick for him. "Hey, Chuck!" He stopped him. "Could you spare me a minute?"

The boy looked trapped.

"I have some Gatorade in the car. I'd like to talk to you."

Slick with sweat from his row, strands of blond hair stuck to his forehead. "Let me shower first," he said.

Fenimore nodded. But he didn't leave and go to his car. He hovered near the base of the staircase, in case his prey decided to bolt.

Fifteen minutes later, Chuck reappeared in jeans and a T-shirt, his backpack dangling from one shoulder. He didn't greet Fenimore, or speak to him on the walk to the car. Traffic had picked up on Kelly Drive and they had to wait for the light.

"Beautiful day." Fenimore attempted to break the awkward silence.

Chuck nodded. His interest in the weather was zero, Fenimore decided. Once in the car, each clutching a cup of Gatorade, Fenimore opened a window. He felt a desperate need for air before he began. The silence had grown, until it seemed like a third person sitting between them. An obese person.

Fenimore didn't know how to begin. And he realized the young man beside him was not going to help him. Chuck glanced at his watch. *He probably has an eight o'clock class,* Fenimore thought. "I can drive you to class."

"No thanks," the boy said. "There's a bus at seven thirty."

Fenimore looked at the dashboard clock. It read seven fifteen. "You know why I asked you here," he plunged in.

Chuck stared stoically through the windshield at the cherry trees in full bloom, but Fenimore doubted if he saw them. "I wanted to remind you what a full life has to offer and ask you to rethink the risk you're taking, if you persist in racing at Henley." He sounded pompous, even to himself.

The boy continued to stare straight ahead. Fenimore detected no change in his expression. "You were lucky last week. But you may not be so lucky next time." He felt foolish, as if he were talking to a statue. He forced himself to go on. "Right now, winning at Henley seems like the most important thing in the world. And it *is* important, of course. It's a tremendous achievement to have come this far in such a demanding sport. But a long life has much to offer, too—a rewarding career, marriage, children, travel, hobbies. . . ." He wasn't even making a dent. Suppressing a strong desire to shake the boy, he tried again. "See those cherry trees!" He waved at the trees. "Don't you want to see them next year? And the year after?" He was shouting. "Look at me, Chuck."

Reluctantly, the boy turned his head.

"Do you really want to risk your life for a boat race?"

It was as if Fenimore had pressed a button and brought a mannequin to life. Chuck's face flushed and his eyes blazed. "We all die," he said. "Remember the Iraqi who risked his life to go to the polls?"

Fenimore nodded.

"When they asked him why he did it, he said, 'Everybody dies. At least I will have died for *something*.'"

"But that's different!" Fenimore cried. "He risked his life for a great cause—*freedom.* You'll be risking yours for . . . for a cup!"

"No!" For the first time the boy looked Fenimore full in the eyes, and when he spoke he stressed each word: *"For being the best I can be."*

Silence filled the car, but this time it wasn't inert and obese. It was alive and palpitating. Fenimore watched Chuck place his cup of Gatorade, still half-full, in the cup holder—sloshing the liquid because his hand was shaking. He unfolded his legs and eased

85

himself out of the car. Before shutting the door, he leaned in and said, "Thanks for the drink."

After all, Chuck had gone to the best schools, and he came from one of the best Philadelphia families, you would expect him to have good manners. *But,* Fenimore asked himself, *where had he learned the rest?*

CHAPTER 21

Deeply depressed by his failure with Chuck, Fenimore returned to his office. Still wearing his rowing clothes, he decided he might as well do a few push-ups before changing. Maybe the exercise would improve his mood. The office was deserted, except for Sal. The cat observed his calisthenics with a speculative expression before settling down on the windowsill for her morning nap.

After a fifteen-minute workout, Fenimore collapsed in his desk chair, breathing heavily. But he didn't dare rest long. It was nearly time for his nurse to arrive, and he didn't want to cause her another conniption fit with his half-naked form. He hurried upstairs to change.

When he reached the second floor, however, he kept going—up to the attic. On an impulse, he wanted to read that poem of Housman's on cherry trees again. He wanted to refresh his memory of one part. He found the book and quickly flipped through *Snyder and Martin* to "Loveliest of Trees," and read the last verse.

> *And since to look at things in bloom*
> *Fifty springs are little room.*

Perhaps if he had been able to quote that verse to Chuck, verbatim . . . No. He shook his head. It wouldn't have made any difference. He sighed. The boy had made up his mind.

Fenimore had barely returned to his office, fully dressed, when the phone rang. Mrs. Doyle answered it. "For you, Doctor. A Myra Henderson." She handed him the receiver.

"How are you, Mrs. Henderson?"

"Myra. Fit as a fiddle. I'm not calling for your medical advice. I need another kind of help."

"I'd be happy to—"

"The public hearing on the marina is being held at City Hall today. Charlie is getting up a crowd of his cronies to support us. I'm bringing as many Historical Society members as I can dig up, and I wondered if you could bring some people along to swell the crowd."

"I'll do my best. When and where do you want them?"

"Two o'clock, in City Hall Courtyard."

"Oh my. I have a full schedule this afternoon."

"Can't you change it? This is important."

"Why didn't Charlie call me before?"

"Oh—didn't you know?"

"Know what?"

"You're persona non grata."

"Oh."

"He's not speaking to you. He asked me to call you."

"I see. Well, I'll try to juggle things. Maybe I can persuade Mrs. Doyle and Horatio to come too."

"Capital."

"Capital?"

"That's what my dear husband, the judge, used to say when he was pleased."

"Did he say that in court?"

"Mercy, no. They might have thought he was referring to the crime."

Fenimore suppressed a laugh. Then he said, "Capital! I'll see you in court . . . er . . . the court*yard*."

When Fenimore told Mrs. Doyle about the protest rally, her eyes lit up. She thought it was a wonderful idea and agreed to help marshal some troops. Although she and her husband had never had any children of their own, Mrs. Doyle came from a huge family full of nieces, nephews, and cousins—first, second, and third, and once, twice, and three times removed. She put in a few calls before the first patient arrived and reported to Fenimore that there would be plenty of people at the hearing. They might not fully understand the cause, but they were warm bodies with strong voices, and that's what counted at a protest.

Fenimore's other employee was not as enthusiastic, however. Even though the rally would mean escaping work, he declined to go.

"Why, Rat?"

"'Cause I think the marina would be great. They said on TV last night they were gonna have all this cool stuff: movies, video games, a pool—even a skateboard arena!"

Fenimore and Doyle shuddered.

"Well, if that's the way you feel," Fenimore said, "you can stay in the office and cover the phone."

Horatio grunted.

CHAPTER 22

City Hall is a Philadelphia institution. Topped by the figure of the Quaker founder, William Penn, it has occupied the center of the city—where Broad and Market Streets cross—since 1884. This Victorian structure was once ridiculed as a public eyesore, with its cupids and gargoyles, its curlicues and furbelows. But today it is cherished and coddled and cleaned with a fervor unknown in the past.

Fenimore and his entourage (he and Mrs. Doyle had persuaded a half-dozen patients to join them—the less sickly ones) piled into the courtyard through the west side archway, bearing a sign (concocted by Doyle from a piece of cardboard attached to a yardstick) which read:

DOWN WITH MARINA!
UP WITH BOATHOUSE ROW!

As they bustled in, Fenimore caught sight of Charlie, who seemed to have the entire Union League in tow. At least he was surrounded by a large group of men sporting Brooks Brothers suits and regimental striped ties.

Just then, there was a commotion at the north archway, and Mrs. Henderson swept in, flanked by several scholarly young people and a large group of plump, gray-haired dowagers. Spying Fenimore, she came up briskly. "You and Charlie and I must leave this gang and go to the hearing in room thirteen where we can state our case."

Fenimore passed this news on to his nurse.

"Don't worry, Doctor," she assured him. "The Doyles can handle this end of it." Surrounded by hordes of Irish faces, all bearing a faint resemblance to Mrs. Doyle, Fenimore felt a quiver of alarm—especially when he glimpsed a few of her burly nephews.

"No rough stuff, now," he warned.

"Saint's honor." Mrs. Doyle crossed herself. "Unless *they* start it," she muttered to herself. She had caught sight of Newborn, the wily developer whose picture she had seen in *The Inquirer*. He was waving a much more elegant sign than hers:

BRING THE SCHULKILL
INTO THE 21ST CENTURY!

He had left the *y* out of Schuylkill, she was happy to see. I'll bring *him* into the twenty-first century—*feet first*, she thought. But she said, "Now run along, Doctor."

The threesome—Fenimore, Charlie, and Mrs. Henderson—made their way through the throng. Mrs. Henderson occupied the middle spot, acting as a buffer between the two men. Room 13 was packed. Two police officers guarded the door.

"Stand back. No room. You can watch it on TV tonight," one officer cried. He had never met Mrs. Henderson.

"Young man!" She pounded her cane. "I'm president of the Pennsylvania Historical Society and I have reserved three seats in the front row."

"ID," he said curtly.

She promptly pushed her passport under his nose. She had never acquired a driver's license because she had always employed a chauffeur.

He glanced at it and let her through. She beckoned to Fenimore and Charlie.

"Just a minute. Who are these—?"

"Dr. Charles Ashburn and Dr. Andrew Fenimore, both highly respected physicians at the Pennsylvania Hospital—and friends of mine."

"IDs," he repeated, but a little less belligerently.

The two doctors dug out their driver's licenses.

The officer scanned them and, with a shrug, let them pass.

If Ashburn and Fenimore had been on more friendly terms, they would have shared a laugh over their lady friend's tactics. As it was, they made their way silently through the congested room to their seats.

The meeting was slow to start, and Fenimore had plenty of time to take in his surroundings. Dingy crystal chandeliers hung from the high ceilings, dusty red carpets covered the floor, mottled green blinds were drawn down tightly over the tall windows, shutting out all natural light. A dais with a heavy mahogany table dominated the front of the room. Behind the table sat a dozen people, men and women in various poses of tension and relaxation—all members of the City Planning Commission. Fenimore wondered which were friends and which were foes. He had barely absorbed all this grimy grandeur, when a bearlike man with a bald pate rose and called the meeting to order. Mrs. Henderson nudged Fenimore and whispered, "That's Wormwood, the man we're after." She had a mean glint in her eye.

Suddenly, Fenimore relaxed. With this lady on their side they had nothing to worry about.

CHAPTER 23

Commissioner Wormwood opened the hearing by introducing the members of the Planning Commission. First he called on Mariah Grub, a fuzzy-haired woman who looked as if she'd just gotten out of bed and had slept in her clothes. She presented the Commission's side of the debate. She did so in an irritating mumble, stressing that there was nothing new about commercial establishments on the Schuylkill. As far back as the 1700s there had been numerous inns and taverns lining the river, serving the traditional catfish and waffles, washed down with grog and mint juleps, depending on the season. (Laughter from the audience.)

Jack Newborn, the developer, was called on next. Stocky and electric, he presented his case in a rapid-fire manner, using numerous charts, diagrams, and slides that nobody understood. But he made the point that river traffic was actually much heavier in the old days, when steamboats plied the Schuylkill packed with pleasure seekers and he pointed out how a modern marina would draw people and revenue into the city.

William Ott, the chief architect of the marina, claimed, in a leisurely drawl, that his design would be as great an addition to the riverbank as the Water Works had been in 1815. And he quoted Charles Dickens on that structure: "The Water Works . . . are no less ornamental than useful, being tastefully laid out as a public garden."

All the promoters of the marina swore that this new development would be a gold-plated asset for Philadelphia, enticing tourists and cash to swell the city's coffers. When they subsided to faint applause, Commissioner Wormwood opened the hearing to the audience. Mrs. Henderson, despite her arthritic hip, leapt to her feet and began:

"'Schuylkill' comes from a Dutch word meaning 'hidden river.' It was called this because the mouth of the river was hidden from the early settlers by bulrushes. Clear and pure, the river abounded with many varieties of fish, and its banks were populated by all kinds of birds and animals. The Lenape Indians made their homes in caves along the banks, and William Penn paddled up the river in a canoe and praised its beauty. The so-called 'commercial establishments' that Mr. Newborn described were quiet country inns, peopled by fishermen and gentry.

"After the Industrial Revolution, when Pennsylvania was full of factories, the river went through a bad time. It was polluted with chemicals and sludge, the result of factory owners allowing refuse to be dumped indiscriminately into the river. The fish died and much of the wildlife disappeared. But, in recent years, Philadelphia has reclaimed the river by dredging and cracking down on the polluters. The only things that disturb the Schuylkill today are the fish, the mallards, and the gentle sweep of rowers' oars. No, I'm wrong," she corrected herself. "Recently *The Inquirer* reported that an otter was seen for the first time in many years, diving from the bank!" She paused dramatically. "And, best of all, Boathouse Row, that beautiful stretch of Victorian architecture that enhances the river with its picturesque lighting every evening, will soon be registered as a historic landmark." Turning, she fixed her piercing gaze on the audience. "Do we really want to change this beautiful, natural waterway into a commercial tourist attraction?" Mrs. Henderson sat down to a burst of wild applause.

Fenimore was the last to stop clapping.

Charlie spoke next. He gave an impassioned plea for the preservation of the boathouses and the sport of rowing. "Rowing is an institution in Philadelphia. In 1835 the first race was held between bargemen: The Imps and the Blue Devils. The Imps wore red and white stripes and the Blue Devils, of course, wore blue jerseys. The Devils won. In 1859 the first college crew was organized by the University of Pennsylvania. During the sesquicentennial, spectators came in droves in their carriages and on horseback, to cheer the oarsmen on. And Thomas Eakins immortalized rowing in his famous painting *Max Schmitt in a Single Scull.* Jack Kelley strengthened the sport by winning worldwide competitions, and later, his son, Jack Jr., won the coveted Diamond Sculls at Henley. Both these men promoted rowing as a way to build character as well as fitness in young men—two qualities we desperately need today."

Fenimore looked away. How could Charlie wax so eloquently on character and fitness when he was sacrificing his own son's health for—a cup?

"Boathouse Row was home to these great men. Are we really going to let these people destroy it?" He gestured at the people on the dais. Ott wore a sneer and Newborn looked as if he would like to jump off the dais and strangle him.

Someone booed and all hell broke loose at the back of the room.

"Down with marinas! Up with boathouses!" chanted the demonstrators.

"Down!"

"Up!"

Fenimore craned his neck, half expecting to see his nurse leading the fray. But the police had already cleared the room.

Commissioner Wormwood wiped his brow and opened the floor to anyone who wished to speak. Fenimore was so moved he jumped to his feet. He described an experience he once had on an Amtrak train, when passengers on the other side of his car had rushed across the aisle to look out the window. "At first, I thought, *terrorists?*" (laughter.) "But no, they just wanted to glimpse our beautiful boathouses, aglow in the dark! Talk about tourist attractions!" He sat down amid cheers.

Fenimore was followed by the presidents of the Fairmount Park Commission, the Park House Association, and the University of Pennsylvania. He looked at his watch. Time to go. He had hospital rounds and patients to see. He wondered if Mrs. Doyle was still here or if she had been arrested for instigating that rumpus at the back of the room. He wouldn't be surprised. Maybe he would have to bail her out. He excused himself to Mrs. Henderson, nodded to Charlie, who ignored him, and irritated a number of people by crawling past them to the end of the row.

When he stepped into the courtyard, he found it deserted except for a homeless man wrapped in a rug, a trickle of pedestrians, and a few pigeons. No sign of Doyle—or her extended family. He gave the homeless man a dollar, paid the fortune he owed to the parking garage, and drove to the hospital. As he drove, he wondered what the outcome of the hearing would be. But he was optimistic. He was betting on Mrs. Henderson and Mrs. Doyle. With those two battle-axes on their side, how could they lose?

When Fenimore arrived home, he found Horatio waiting for him.

"What's up, Rat?"

"It's Tanya."

"What . . . ?"

"She's got this lousy cough."

Fenimore felt a wave of guilt. He should have done something about her sooner. "Bring her over tonight. I'll take a look at her."

"What if a cop spots her?"

Fenimore was taken aback. He hadn't thought of that. "You'd better bring her after dark—and disguise her somehow."

He nodded. "Leave it to me."

Fenimore did. He knew Horatio's skills at disguises. With a few items garnered from a thrift shop, he had once changed Fenimore from a respectable physician into a street thug. He pictured Tanya arriving in a burka.

CHAPTER 24

Spurred by Horatio's report, Fenimore went upstairs to examine his two spare bedrooms—one for Tanya, one for her baby-sitter. *Thank heavens these brownstones were roomy,* he thought. But to his dismay he found that his rooms, although large, were shabby and in disrepair. The ceiling of one bore ugly brown stains from a leak in the roof and the floorboards in the other had buckled in places from the damp.

Where will I find time to do these repairs?

Hold on, Fenimore. This child has been living in a cellar, filled with refuse and rats. To her, either of these rooms will seem like paradise. And as for Jennifer, it's not as if she hasn't slept here before. She knows what to expect, and she's not exactly a neat freak. And Mrs. Lopez can't be too finicky after living with Horatio all these years.

Fenimore vacuumed and dusted, made up the beds, and laid out fresh towels. Feeling calmer, he went to the telephone. He called Doyle first.

"She won't be any trouble," he explained. "All you have to do is keep an eye on her, see that she eats a nutritious lunch and doesn't leave the house. Why, most thirteen-year-olds are baby-sitters themselves, so it should be easy."

"Huh."

With that single syllable, Doyle conveyed to Fenimore how little he knew about teenagers. But as soon as she heard Tanya's history, she was more than willing to help.

Jennifer was a different story.

"Oh, Andrew," she said as soon as she heard his voice. "I was just about to call you. I'm going to be out of town this weekend."

"Oh?"

"I'm going to South Jersey to work on my book."

"Your what?"

"Remember Roaring Wings?"

"How could I forget him?" Roaring Wings was the formidable brother of Sweet Grass, the victim of a murder that Fenimore had solved. One of the last chiefs of the Lenape tribe, he had little patience with the *wasechus* (white man) and made no attempt to hide his disdain for him. Fenimore was no exception.

"Well, he called me last night," Jennifer went on, "and asked how I was getting on with my book about the Lenapes. . . ."

To Fenimore's knowledge, Jennifer had not written a word about the Lenapes. "So, what did you tell him?"

"I thought fast and told him it was still in the research stage and I'd like to come down and interview him."

"Quick thinking."

"He sounded very pleased."

"A first for Roaring Wings," Fenimore muttered.

"I'm going down on Saturday to talk to him."

"I see." He detected an underlying excitement in her voice that was disturbing. He realized he hadn't heard it for some time.

"What's wrong?" she asked, sensing his disappointment.

"Nothing. I was hoping you could teen-sit this weekend. Tanya, Horatio's homeless friend, is moving in on Saturday."

"Oh, I am sorry. Maybe I could change—"

"No. We'll manage," Fenimore said heroically.

"I'm really excited. I'm taking a tape recorder along."

"Do you think he'll go for that?"

"Probably not, but it's worth a try. I don't know shorthand."

"Have you ever interviewed anyone?"

"No."

"Well, be sure to prepare a good list of questions."

"I've already started. Dad has a wonderful library on the Lenapes."

"Well . . . good luck."

"Thanks. And I'm sorry I can't help out."

Fenimore called Doyle back.

"Don't worry, Doctor," she said cheerfully. "I'll be glad to come for the weekend. Just be sure your TV is working."

"Bless you," Fenimore said.

Having solved that crisis, Fenimore was feeling good, except for a tiny gnawing doubt about Jennifer. Rafferty's warning came back to him. Had he been taking her too much for granted? He ate a lonely dinner of lowfat ham on rye, washed down with a Diet Coke. By using paper plates and cups, he had managed to reduce his dishwashing chores to a minimum. He was washing his single utensil—the knife he had used to spread the mustard—when the doorbell rang.

CHAPTER 25

Fenimore peered through the frosted glass panels of his Victorian front door and was surprised to see another youth with Horatio. Slighter and shorter, but with the same dress code—baggy pants, T-shirt, baseball cap worn in reverse. Where was Tanya? He opened the door.

Casting a quick glance up and down the street, Horatio shoved his companion into the vestibule. In the stronger light of the hall, it was obvious that the youth's features were too delicate for a boy's, and even though the T-shirt was two sizes too big, certain curves were discernable underneath.

"Come in. Come in." Fenimore's shyness emerged in the form of brusqueness. He didn't know many teenage girls. Most of his female patients were sixty-five or over.

As soon as she was inside, Tanya yanked off her cap, letting an abundance of thick, dark hair fall to her shoulders. "Geez, Rat. That hat was squeezin' my brains to death."

"If you had any," Rat said.

She jabbed him with her elbow.

He feigned mortal injury.

Thus Fenimore was introduced to teenage courtship for the

first time. The performance was interrupted by Tanya, who broke into a violent fit of coughing. Fenimore hurried her into his inner office, and asked Horatio to leave while he examined her.

The minute they were alone, Fenimore sensed the young woman's tension. He knew he should have a female chaperone. Especially in light of the child's history. He cursed himself for not having Doyle there. But he had to listen to her chest. And he couldn't do it adequately unless she removed her shirt. He told her to go into the examining room and take off her T-shirt.

When he entered, she had removed her shirt and was holding it over her small breasts. Adopting his most professional manner— no small talk, no jokes—he said, "This may be cold," and pressed the metal disk of his stethoscope against her bare back. His nervousness was instantly replaced by concern. He heard definite rales, and when he asked her to cough for him she went into a spasm that continued until he brought her a glass of water and cough syrup with codeine. There was no need to listen to her chest. Fenimore had learned all he needed to know. He said, "Your cold has turned into something more serious. I'm prescribing an antibiotic, and you must get plenty of rest."

She looked alarmed.

"You'll be fine in a few days," he assured her. "Rat and I, and my nurse, Mrs. Doyle, will take good care of you."

It was Tanya's turn to look nervous. "I can't pay you anything."

"Don't worry. I'll take it out of Rat's pay." He winked. "He works for me, you know."

She smiled for the first time. "He won't like that."

"I know." He smiled back. He told her to put on her shirt, and left the room.

He found Rat in the outer office, reading a medical journal. He read them often, and afterward, to Fenimore's amazement, asked intelligent questions about the articles. Fenimore told the boy about Tanya's condition. "She can't go back to that cellar tonight. She has to stay here. And you'll have to be her chaperone."

"Huh?"

"I know, it's crazy, but these are the times we live in. You can sleep on the couch. You'd better call your mother."

While Horatio made his call, Fenimore took Tanya upstairs and introduced her to her new quarters. She was thrilled. The clean white sheets were what attracted her most. She ran her hand lightly over them, as if the plain cotton were satin or silk and buried her face in the pillow. He showed her the bathroom down the hall. Horatio joined them, and watched his friend's face with pleasure as she reacted to her new surroundings.

"Uh . . . do you have a nightgown?" Fenimore asked, hesitantly.

"My mom gave her one of hers," Horatio said. He tossed a grocery bag with the nightgown at Tanya. She caught it.

"What about a toothbrush?"

The boy drew a new one from his pocket and flipped it at her. She dropped it.

"Butterfingers!"

Rat had thought of everything. Fenimore wondered when the girl had last brushed her teeth. For someone who had lived in a cellar for over six weeks, they looked remarkably clean. Then it dawned on him that she had been clean when he had examined her. She had no body odor, and when he had bent to listen to her lungs, her hair had smelled of shampoo. After Tanya had taken her antibiotic and gone to bed, Fenimore confronted Horatio.

"I took her to my house first," he said, "and my mom helped her clean up. Tan wouldn't come to see you—dirty."

He patted the boy's shoulder. "You've taken good care of her, Rat." Fenimore had thought of asking Mrs. Lopez to take the girl in, but then he had remembered that she worked full-time and the two teenagers would be alone all day—at least in the summer. Besides, she had a limited income and didn't need another mouth to feed.

Embarrassed by the doctor's praise, Rat grabbed the blanket and pillow that Fenimore had brought down for him, threw himself on the sofa, and picked up the TV remote. Sal curled up beside him.

"You know where the fridge is," Fenimore said.

Horatio grunted.

Fenimore returned to his room. Unaccustomed to having a full house, and missing Sal's company, he slept fitfully.

CHAPTER 26

Saturday began quietly enough.

Fenimore overslept. Something he rarely did. Probably due to his restless night. By the time he dressed and arrived downstairs, Rat had purchased coffee and bagels from a deli on the corner and was passing them out.

Tanya was wearing the same clothes as the night before.

"We'll have to get you some new clothes, young lady," Fenimore said.

She looked down at her outfit. "What's wrong with these?"

"Yeah, Doc. What's wrong with those? I took a lot of pains with that outfit." Rat looked at Tanya appraisingly.

"I'm sure you did. But she'll need more than one ensemble."

"En—what?"

"Outfit."

"Okay. Sure. But if you're gonna take Tan shoppin', I'm coming with you," he said. "Or she'll end up looking like a nun in lace-ups."

"Lace-ups!" she gasped.

"Yeah, and I don't mean sneakers."

"Oow." She screwed up her face.

"He might even make you wear a bra."

Tanya blushed.

So did Fenimore. "That's enough, Rat. You can come along if you want, but you have to behave yourself."

He shrugged, falling into his standard tough-guy stance.

Tanya began to cough. When she recovered, Fenimore said, "There will be no shopping until you're all well. Why don't you lie down on the couch and watch TV while Rat and I get to work."

Office hours were about to begin and Mrs. Doyle would be arriving any minute. Rat set the TV to the Cartoon Channel for Tanya. Mrs. Doyle came in with her overnight bag and the latest *TV Guide* under one arm. Rat introduced Tanya to the nurse. Rat and Doyle went to work in the office. Fenimore took care of his morning patients and went to the hospital to do his rounds. He wondered briefly how Jennifer was making out with Roaring Wings. (Poor choice of words!) How her interview was going. When he returned, Doyle had prepared a healthy lunch for the four of them: chicken sandwiches, fruit cups, and iced tea. Tanya only coughed once during the meal. After lunch, Sal put her stamp of approval on the new guest by curling up beside her on the sofa. Fenimore suggested that Tanya take a nap. Horatio plumped a pillow behind her head. The warmth of the look she sent him in return did not escape Fenimore. *Young love,* he thought wistfully, and returned to his office.

He was daydreaming at his desk when the phone rang, startling him. Since Doyle was there, he let her answer it. He couldn't hear her words through the door, but he sensed her alarm. A moment later she burst in.

"It was Mrs. Ashburn. Chuck collapsed during rowing practice. He's in Emergency at HUP. She wants you to come!"

HUP was its usual chaotic self. A vendor was selling melons from the back of a ramshackle truck at one entrance. The main lobby was full of people milling around, chatting, reading, sleeping, and chasing after their children.

Fenimore automatically made his way through the mêleé to the elevators. He could have come in the back entrance, but his mind was so absorbed with Chuck he simply forgot. The Cardiac Care Unit was on the eighth floor. He got off with a young woman and an elderly couple, and wondered, fleetingly, who they were coming to visit. Fenimore was used to visiting the CCU at his own hospital. He did so every day. But as a doctor, not as a family friend. It made a difference. A small group was gathered outside in the corridor: Frank O'Brien, Henry Walsh, and a few rowers, still in their rowing attire. Only immediate family members were allowed in the CCU. A young man, probably a resident, was speaking to them quietly as Fenimore came up. He told Fenimore to go right in.

The CCU was as busy as the lobby, but the personnel—doctors, nurses, technicians, and orderlies—moved with purpose, sure of their errands. The chief cardiologist was standing on one side of Chuck's bed; Caroline and Charlie were on the other. The cardiologist nodded at Fenimore. Caroline glanced up and gave a wan smile. Charlie's gaze was riveted to his son's face. The father's face, usually ruddy, was putty-colored. Chuck lay supine, eyes closed, his complexion ashen. A nurse was deftly connecting him to an echocardiograph machine. Fenimore glanced at the EKG above the boy's head and saw that nothing much was going on. The rate was fast, but the tracing looked normal. Before he had a chance to speak to the Ashburns, the cardiologist signaled him to join him in the corridor.

"A strange business," he said.

"What happened?"

He told Fenimore, "Chuck was coming into the dock after his practice, when he collapsed. Just slumped over his oars. He was in a singles, and by the time some of the crew members reached him, he was unconscious. Two of the boys took turns giving him

CPR until the ambulance came, but he didn't regain consciousness."

"What tests have been done?"

"A cardiogram, a blood count, SMA-12, and electrolytes, and they're about to do an echo." The doctor drew Fenimore down the hall, away from the people outside the CCU, who were staring at them. He spoke in a hushed tone. "There's something odd about this case, Fenimore."

"In what way?"

"It seems he's an SCD candidate. He has an ICD implant. The coach brought the boy's wallet in and we found his interrogation card. But when we interrogated the ICD there was no sign of a cardiac event at any time."

"Are you sure?" Fenimore shouldn't have said that. It was insulting. But the doctor, intent on the case, took no offense. "Was the ICD functioning properly?" Fenimore asked.

"Perfectly."

"You're suggesting his collapse was caused by something else."

The other doctor nodded. "We'll know more when we have the lab tests."

"How soon will that be?"

"About an hour. Mrs. Ashburn said you were an old family friend, and I thought you should know."

"I appreciate it."

The doctor excused himself.

Fenimore wasn't sure what to do next. He couldn't help the Ashburns until he saw the results of the lab tests. And he didn't want to get involved with the group in the corridor. He looked at his watch. 1:45. He remembered it was Saturday and there should be a cardiology lecture. Scheduled each week, these lectures were open to HUP alumni who wanted to keep up in their specialties. Many were from out-of-town. He decided to check out the auditorium. As he made his way to another part of the hospital, he spied a familiar face. Ott—the architect for the marina. What was he doing here? Oh . . . he was probably on the faculty at the architecture school. But that was on the other side of campus. So what, Fenimore. People are allowed to cross the campus. He quickened his steps. If he was going to go to the lecture, he might as well be on time.

CHAPTER 27

Fenimore arrived at the auditorium a few minutes early. While waiting—and to take his mind off Chuck—he browsed among the display cases in the hall. One case contained an ornate brass doorknob that had opened the door of the first hospital in Pennsylvania in 1752. Another displayed reproductions of two famous paintings by Thomas Eakins—*The Gross Clinic* and *The Agnew Clinic*. In the first, the surgeon was clad in dark street clothes; in the second the surgeon wore white—a sign that during the interim, bacteria had been discovered and aseptic surgery had come into its own. Fenimore was about to head back to the lecture hall when a quote, neatly typed on a white card, caught his eye:

"The bedside study of disease, and the personal familiarity of the student with its manifold symptoms, can alone make the competent and skilled physician, and is justly regarded as the capping stone of a complete medical education."

George W. F. Norris, M.D.
Professor of Ophthalmology, 1897

Capping stone, indeed, thought Fenimore. *That was over a hundred years ago. Today we feed symptoms into a computer and diagnose the disease from a printout. The patient still lies in a bed, but, sadly, the bedside is often empty.* Shaking his head, he returned to the auditorium.

Most of the seats were occupied, but the lecture had not begun. Fenimore scanned the audience for familiar faces. He waved to one. Then he spotted another at the back of the room. Daniel Burton, the doctor from Pine Lake, was just arriving. He remembered Burton telling him, during his examination, that he tried to get to these lectures. "When you live in the boonies, you have to make an effort to keep up," he had said. Fenimore wondered if he knew about Chuck. He tried to think of a way to break the news without revealing the extent of his own friendship with the Ashburns. He went up to him and said casually, "Did you hear about Ashburn's son? You know Chuck, right?"

He nodded. "What happened?"

"He collapsed during rowing practice. He's in the CCU. They found he has an ICD implant, but when they interrogated it they found no evidence of cardiomyopathy."

The doctor, to Fenimore's surprise, appeared deeply distraught. Burton had not struck Fenimore as a particularly sensitive guy. "He's doing okay, though," he said hastily. "They were getting ready to do an echocardiogram when I left."

"What should I do?" he asked. "Should I go over there?"

"Why don't you wait until after the lecture. The lab tests should be back then, and you can take a look at them," Fenimore said kindly.

Looking relieved, Burton took one of the last remaining seats in the rear. Fenimore found one up front just before the lights went down. Apparently, this lecture included slides.

It was a long, esoteric dissertation by an archeologist on the possible cardiac condition of King Tut in 1352 B.C. Fenimore had trouble concentrating, his mind returning again and again to Chuck and what the cardiologist had told him. If the boy's collapse had not been caused by a cardiac event, what had caused it? His mind ran over the list of possibilities. Sunstroke, hyperthermia, hypoglycemia, seizure . . . But there were no signs or symptoms for any of these conditions. Fenimore suppressed a groan as another slide appeared. At least this one was right side up. He glanced at his watch. He had been here well over an hour. He was contemplating sneaking out when the lecture abruptly ended and the lights came up. Amid the smattering of applause, Fenimore made his way to the back of the room. As he approached Burton, the doctor gave a big yawn indicating his opinion of the lecture. Fenimore smiled in agreement.

"Whenever there's a sleeper like this, I wonder why I bother," Burton said.

"I know what you mean. I think I'll go down to the river and take a row to wake me up. But first, let's see Ashburn."

"You know, Fenimore, I think I'd better get back. I didn't know this would go on so long and I have patients to see at home. Could you ask the attending cardiologist to send me a report?"

"I'd be glad to."

"Thanks. I'll call Charlie tonight." He dug his briefcase from under the seat and hurried out.

Fenimore scratched his head, wondering at this sudden change of mind. He finally decided Burton was one of those guys who avoided unpleasant situations whenever possible. Then why had he become a doctor? But Fenimore had more pressing things to think about. He made his way back to the CCU.

The cluster of concerned friends had vanished, but as Fenimore entered, pandemonium reigned. A nurse pulled him aside. "It's the Ashburn boy."

Careful to keep out of the way of doctors, nurses, and technicians, Fenimore edged toward Chuck's bed. As he drew near, he saw a technician unhook the boy from the electrocardiograph machine and remove his IV lines. He turned away sharply as she drew the sheet over his face.

He looked around. Where were Caroline and Charlie? Nowhere in sight. He stopped a passing resident. "Where are the Ashburns?"

He paused. "Went for coffee, I guess."

"You mean, they don't know?"

"I don't think so. It all happened so fast."

Oh my God. Fenimore rushed out, grabbed the first down elevator, and headed for the cafeteria.

They were at the back of the noisy, cavernous room, huddled over their coffee cups. It actually occurred to Fenimore that he didn't have to do this. They hadn't seen him yet. Someone else could do it when they returned to the CCU. A nurse or an intern. Someone not emotionally involved. He could turn around right now and walk out.

A nurse knocked his elbow with her overloaded tray. *A nurse should know better than to eat so much,* he thought inconsequentially. The knock triggered him into action. He approached the Ashburns' table.

Caroline looked up, and Fenimore was spared words. His expression had conveyed his news without speaking. She stumbled to her feet, rattling the coffee cups. Charlie turned to see what had upset her. When he saw Fenimore, he also rose.

"I'm so terribly sor—" Fenimore began.

They turned away, toward each other, and fell into a clumsy embrace.

CHAPTER 28

Fenimore's only desire was to get away, out of the hospital. He blinked as he stepped from the dim, stale lobby into the brilliant spring afternoon. The sycamores along Spruce Street strutted their crowns of new green leaves. The tulips and daffodils displayed their bright hues along the curbs, in pots and window boxes. The mingled scents of cherry blossoms, lilacs, and newly cut grass wafted from the Penn campus nearby.

It's obscene, Fenimore thought—when Chuck has just died!

Amazed at the depth of his feelings, he tried to imagine what the Ashburns were feeling. He hoped they were beyond feeling. Numb. Comatose. Oh, how he hoped that!

In an attempt to ignore the burgeoning life around him, Fenimore bent his gaze on the dirty cement sidewalk and deliberately inhaled the noxious fumes of a passing bus. "Even in the city," he moaned, "spring breathes her sweet breath into the darkest corners and crevices, the meanest backyards and alleyways. There's no escape." Before crossing Spruce Street, he was forced to look up at the traffic light and was struck by a cruel sight. On the opposite corner, a young couple waiting for the same light, their arms entwined, gazed at each other in an ecstasy of love and spring fever.

When the light changed, Fenimore hurried past them, eyes averted, and was glad when he reached his car and could shut himself up inside—away from all signs of spring.

He maneuvered his car onto Chestnut Street and headed downtown with no special destination in mind. His only thought was to lose his thoughts in the chaos of the early commuter traffic.

By the time Fenimore reached Twentieth Street, he had recovered enough to remember his former intention to go for a row. The quiet of the river had always soothed his nerves in the past; maybe it would work today. Instead of continuing downtown to his office, he made a left and headed for the parkway. He had shoved a change of clothes into his trunk, on an impulse, a few days ago for just such an emergency. They would come in handy now.

He changed quickly, fetched his oars and his shell, and set his shell in the water. He slipped his feet into the shoes attached to the bottom and settled onto the seat. He was reaching for the oars when a voice called, "Hey, Doc."

He turned to see Hank Walsh about to take off in his shell. He debated whether to tell him about Chuck. Since they were both in their shells and could only communicate by shouting, he decided against it. Why ruin his afternoon? He would learn the terrible news soon enough. Fenimore simply waved, pushed away from the dock, and began to row upriver.

Hank followed Fenimore slowly. Hank was taking it easy. The contest for Henley was over and he could relax. *There was always next year.* But he didn't have to think about that for a while.

Unless Chuck didn't make it.

He shook this bad thought from his head. *Sure, Chuck will make it. I'll go see him tonight.* The fact that he had lost the race for Henley was gradually becoming a reality to Hank. But, after so many months of demanding the best of himself, relaxing didn't come easily. At first he had felt resentful. All his hopes and dreams shattered in a few minutes. *And it had been a close race—a matter of seconds. Was it worth the effort? Sure. Would I try again? Sure. There was always next year,* he repeated. Meanwhile, it was nice to row lazily upriver, smell the cherry blossoms, and watch the reflection of a bird sail across the water.

Fenimore was surprised to see the Falls Bridge looming above him. He hadn't realized he had come so far. Preoccupied with his thoughts, he had not noticed the landscape around him, only the landscape of his mind and emotions. He decided he had better get home and check on his newly adopted family. There might be certain obligations. He turned his shell and, facing upriver, began to row back to the boathouse.

The river was empty except for one other singles shell—a small speck in the distance. Fenimore felt calmer now. The river always had a calming effect on him, unless it was choppy. But he rarely went out in windy weather. He still didn't have complete confidence in his rowing skills. That would come in time. Meanwhile, he wasn't going to take any chances.

By the time he neared Peter's Island, he realized that he had accepted the fact that Chuck would die young the moment the boy had refused to give up Henley. That's why he had been so depressed. But he had expected Chuck to die in a shell—in the midst of a thrilling race—in a blaze of glory! Not in a hospital bed, hooked up to tubes and machines, surrounded by people in rubber-soled shoes.

And there were so many unanswered questions about how Chuck died. He had collapsed while rowing, but not while *racing*. He had been merely practicing, not demanding the best of himself. And why hadn't the ICD registered something? Perhaps the lab reports would answer some of these questions. In his distress over the boy's death, Fenimore had left the hospital without looking at the reports. He must get hold of them immediately.

He had reached the lower end of the island when the motorboat shot out.

Damn fool! What's he doing coming upriver on the east side? And why is his face covered? My God! He's coming right at me!

The last thing Fenimore remembered was a loud crack—and the shock of cold water closing over his head.

Hank was daydreaming. He was thinking that now he would have more time for his girlfriend, Amanda. He let his oar trail in the water and watched the tiny waves eddy around it. He might even take her dancing like she'd been nagging him to do for months. He grinned. But only if she didn't make him wear a tie.

Smack!

What the hell? A rock? He scanned the shore, taking his bearings. He was just south of Peter's Island. *There aren't any rocks here.* He craned his neck around the hull and saw it. *A capsized shell.* He scanned the river for the rower. No one broke the placid surface of the water. He yanked the string that released the Velcro straps on his shoes, rose cautiously, and dove in. He tried to push the other shell with his hands. It wouldn't budge. *That's strange. Singles shells are light, and I'm pretty strong.* He ducked under the shell and opened his eyes.

Through the murky water he made out a rower dangling upside down, his feet still locked in his shoes.

Hank reached up and yanked the string that held the straps, just as he had done with his own shoes. The straps loosened and the rower slipped free. Hank was ready to catch him, but he was unprepared for the impact of his body. It knocked him backward and down. By churning with one arm he managed to hold his own and slowly rise to the surface with his burden. When he broke through the water, he threw his head back and gulped air. Tossing the water from his eyes, he aimed for the island's shore. It was only a couple of yards, but swimming with one arm was hard. *Thank God I'm in shape,* he thought, *or I couldn't do this.* He dragged the man onto the grass and turned him over.

Holy shit!

He began CPR.

Hank had no idea how long the doctor had been underwater— and his expectations for his revival were low.

Press, release, pause. Press, release, pause.

As he worked, he spared a brief thought for the two abandoned shells that were floating downriver—worth eight thousand dollars apiece. Not to mention the oars. Maybe someone would rescue them.

Water gushed from the doctor's mouth after every pressure, but there was less each time.

Hank paused to listen to his chest. Nothing. He felt the carotid artery. Nothing. He went back to work. With no means of transportation, how would he get off the island? It was getting dark. Would he have to spend the night here? *With a dead man?* At this thought, he renewed his efforts.

Press, release, pause. Press, release, pause. He checked the carotid again. Did he detect a faint throbbing?

Fenimore was conscious of severe pain in his abdomen. *He had to stop it.* He opened his eyes to see what was causing it.

A pair of dark eyes, two inches from his nose, stared down at him.

CHAPTER 29

The hospital room was undistinguished except for the abundance of flowers spilling over the windowsill, taking up the table provided for meals, even crowding into the corners. Jennifer and Mrs. Doyle had shoved them aside to prevent the medical staff from tripping over them and breaking their necks. Friends, patients, even one relative—a distant cousin from Saskatchewan whom Fenimore hadn't seen for years—had read about the doctor's accident in some obscure newspaper and remembered him florally.

Accident? Ha! Talk about euphemisms, thought Fenimore. That masked guy had run right into him on purpose. And if it hadn't been for Hank . . . He shuddered. If he could only get out of here, he might be able to find the culprit.

This whole hospitalization was ridiculous. You either drowned or you didn't. What was all this blather about "near drowning"? He felt fine. But his doctor had advised an observation period, because there's this thing called "secondary drowning," in which you can pop off days, even weeks, after your original drowning—the result of some infection, pneumonia, whatever. Of course he knew about this, but it was rare. He thought everyone was being overly cautious. "At your age . . ." was the depressing refrain he kept hearing. Was he really that old? Well, he'd put up with it for a day or two longer. Then he had to get out of here.

After Fenimore had been transferred to the hospital, his first thought had been of Chuck's lab tests. He had to see them. As soon as Mrs. Doyle was allowed to visit, he asked her to please get them for him. Her answer had shocked him.

"Certainly not. You aren't supposed to worry about anything, except getting well." And she was adamant.

"But—"

"Now, what else would you like me to bring? Your PJs, your bathrobe . . . ?" She ticked off a list of totally unnecessary items.

When Jennifer arrived, he asked her to bring one thing—rather, two things—his bedroom slippers. (He knew Doyle wouldn't bring them; she would think them too disreputable.) He hated those paper slippers the hospital supplied.

Every time Doyle appeared, he repeated his request for Chuck's lab report, to no avail. Not until he said, "I'll worry myself sick until I see them," did she finally relent. When she brought them, he tore open the envelope like a man possessed.

Scrawled at the top was a note from the HUP cardiologist whom Fenimore had spoken with at the CCU: "Please take a look at this and give me a call. An autopsy is in the works."

Most of the results were normal, until he reached the last line: serum potassium very low—1.9. The normal range was 3 to 5 milligrams.

Fenimore paused and reread these words. How could Chuck have such low potassium? Did he take something? Or did someone give him something. . . ?

Was Chuck poisoned?

Fenimore felt a little lightheaded himself. He hoped Doyle wasn't right and the lab report had triggered a relapse. He lay still and took deep breaths.

Who would do such a thing? And if he was poisoned, when and how had the poison been introduced? It must have been before Chuck went to practice that afternoon—deposited in his lunch, or maybe someone slipped something in his Gatorade. All the rowers drank that stuff like water. But how would they disguise the taste of such a poisonous cocktail? Surely Chuck would have noticed something. . . .

"Dr. Fenimore . . ." A nurse came in to take his blood pressure and he had to postpone his detecting. That was the trouble with hospitals—they were no place to get any rest. He recalled the old joke about how they woke you up to give you your sleeping pill. He had to make use of every moment of solitude. After dinner, he usually had a half hour to himself before visiting hours began. From the pocket of his new bathrobe, he drew the pen and pad that Jen had kindly brought him. The bathrobe was a gift from Doyle, because, she said, "You can't wear that old rag in the hospital." But Jen had forgotten his dear old slippers, which indicated her mind was elsewhere. She was spending entirely too much time with Roaring Wings.

He was about to write "Suspects" at the top of the page, but cautioned himself. They weren't really suspects. He had no evidence against any of them. They were merely PPIs—People Possibly Implicated.

Stick to the essentials, Fenimore. Who would benefit from Chuck's death?

Hank Walsh.

He will be going to Henley now to compete for the Diamond Sculls, the most coveted prize in the rowing world. (But he saved my life—and he's a nice kid.) Be objective, Fenimore.

Other names quickly followed.

Henry Walsh.

Hank's father would benefit by having such an illustrious son. He could brag about him at his law firm. It was quite an achievement for an African American to compete in what has long been known as an exclusive, white man's sport. It couldn't help but raise his prestige at his firm. And he had been hovering around the ICU when Chuck was there.

Frank O'Brien.

The coach would benefit from Hank's reflected glory, if he sent an African American to Henley. He would have benefited from Chuck's glory as well. But diversity was the big thing now—and Hank's participation would give him a little extra edge over other coaches. Frank had also been in the group hanging around the CCU.

Commissioner Wormwood and the Planning Commission.

Maybe they're all in on it, like in *Murder on the Orient Express*. And that Grub woman from the planning commission heads the list. (But she didn't need to resort to poison. All she had to do was open her mouth and she'd bore you to death.) Seriously, these river accidents could cast an ominous shadow over the whole sport of rowing and provide a reason for destroying Boathouse Row. Didn't Jen say she'd heard somebody talking about an "accident"?

Jack Newborn.

That developer has ants in his pants. Always on the move, ready to change things for the sake of change—or to put more lucre in his pocket. Besides, he has shifty eyes.

William Ott.

Now there's a smarmy fellow. He's so oily he'd slip in his own shoes. And he has everything to gain by getting rid of the boathouses. He could make a real name for himself on that site with his design for a new marina. And didn't I see him prowling around the hospital after Chuck was admitted?

Myra Henderson.

Are you crazy? She's 100 percent behind the boathouses.

Maybe too much behind them? Could that Historical Society be a smoke screen? Maybe she's invested in the marina, under the table. You never know.

Charlie Ashburn.

Now I know you're crazy. You may not see eye to eye with Charlie on some things, but he wouldn't try to murder you. And certainly not his son. *Unless Chuck refused to race for him.* Could my talk actually have made an impression on Chuck, and he told his father he was going to quit?

Caroline Ashburn.

I knew you'd be getting to her. Well, you can cross her off as far as Chuck goes. Mothers simply don't go around murdering their sons. Anyway, I can't think of a single motive. Life insurance? (I'll look into that.) God, Fenimore, have you no heart? Bah humbug. She'd have fewer qualms about bumping me off, I'm sure. But for what motive? Because I tried to keep her from attending tea parties at Henley? Too far-fetched, even for you, Fenimore. Besides, she certainly wasn't steering that motorboat. But she could have hired someone. Money was no object to Caroline.

Is that it? Not quite.

Geoffrey Hunter-Powell.

That snot-nosed British scout. He had everything to gain from eliminating the competition.

Well, that about winds it up. He put down his pen just as Mrs. Doyle bustled into the room, closely followed by Jennifer, Rafferty, and Rat. What ever happened to that golden hospital rule: no more than two visitors at a time?

CHAPTER 30

After three days, Fenimore was released from the hospital, but he was cautioned by his physician to take it easy. He was not to do any physical exercise other than limited walking for at least a month. So much for rowing. But Fenimore's appetite for the river had decreased significantly during the past few days.

On his first day home, Fenimore paid the Walshes a visit. He had called ahead and asked if he could stop by after dinner. Then he had spent the afternoon in a futile search for a gift. He had wandered from department store to sporting goods store to jewelry boutique. But what gift can you give someone who has saved your life? He finally gave up and decided that a few heartfelt words and a strong handshake would convey his feelings better than anything he could buy. He prepared his words carefully as he drove to Germantown.

Feeling empty-handed and awkward, Fenimore rang the bell at the Victorian stone house. The petite woman who had reminded him of a bird at the regatta opened the door.

"Dr. Fenimore!" Mrs. Walsh grasped both his hands and drew him into the living room. Henry Walsh and Hank rose simultaneously from the sofa, where they had been watching a baseball game, and greeted him. All awkwardness was forgotten.

Quickly seated in a soft chair, Fenimore was offered a long list of beverages—from iced tea to Scotch and soda. He wanted Scotch, but since he was driving, he took tea. Henry disappeared to get the drinks and Fenimore decided to save his speech until he came back. But as soon as Henry returned, Hank launched into a detailed description of his rescue of Fenimore—how he'd found him, dragged him from the river, given him CPR, and finally revived him. "I was scared shitless you were going to die on me," the boy said.

"Hush." His mother sent him a look.

Fenimore laughed. "I don't blame you," he said. "I wouldn't want to spend the night on Peter's Island with a corpse."

They all laughed.

The conversation naturally turned to rowing, the recent regatta, Chuck's victory, and, inevitably, the boy's death. The party grew somber. Remembering that he was in the company of two people on his PPI list, Hank and his father, Fenimore observed their reactions carefully as they spoke of Chuck. The distress of both men seemed genuine, and they moved on to other things. There were few pauses in their talk, and whenever Fenimore tried to begin the little thank-you speech he had prepared, Henry or Hank or Mrs. Walsh would bring up a new topic. The evening passed quickly. When Fenimore glanced at the clock on the mantel, it read past eleven. "Mercy, I must be going," he said.

"Yes," Mrs. Walsh quickly agreed. "You must take care of yourself and get plenty of rest."

Fenimore rose and tried once more to make his speech. "Before I go, I want to th—" Again he was cut off. Chatting and laughing, his three hosts escorted him to the door. The next thing he knew, he was standing outside, alone, under a starry sky, his speech still unsaid. Nevertheless, as he drove into the city, he felt content. He knew the Walshes had understood what he had come to say—without words.

When Fenimore arrived home, he had intended to go into his office and cross Henry and Hank Walsh off his PPI list. But he was so tired he went straight to bed.

CHAPTER 31

Mrs. Doyle had taken it upon herself to reduce Fenimore's patient load to a mere trickle, and he found himself at loose ends—pacing his office, browsing through the magazines in the waiting room. (He was beginning to recognize some of the faces in *People*!) He even watched television with Tanya occasionally. (But their tastes differed. Tanya liked *American Idol* and Fenimore preferred the History Channel.) The thought that occupied his mind day and night was Chuck's autopsy report. He couldn't go ahead with his investigation until he saw it. He thought about little else. Every now and then he let thoughts of Jennifer seep in. She hadn't called since he'd been home. You'd think she'd want to know how he was doing. . . .

He tried to divert his mind by reading *JAMA* and *The New England Journal of Medicine,* but the articles seemed longer than usual and he had trouble concentrating on them.

Oh no! He was standing stock still when his nurse came in.

"What's wrong?" she asked sharply.

"Have you noticed anything wrong with my mental abilities since I've been home?" He looked panicky.

"No more than usual," she said briskly. For once her insult was reassuring. "Why do you ask?"

"I thought my attention span was shorter and I might have suffered brain damage while I was unconscious."

"Pshaw! Even if you did, you have plenty to spare."

Did he detect a compliment?

"This report just came." She shoved some papers under his nose.

All worries about his mental deterioration vanished as he stared down at Chuck's autopsy report. He scanned it quickly, for the gist. To his amazement, Chuck's heart and blood vessels were normal. There were no signs of any abnormalities, such as an enlargement of the heart or thickening of the arteries. Why the ICD implant, then?

Fenimore read on. "A blood specimen taken just before the patient died showed an extremely high potassium level—13.6." *My God.* A small amount might have been introduced to correct the effects of the low potassium when he was admitted. But that would have been introduced gradually, over a ten- to twelve-hour period. Such a large amount, introduced all at once, could have been the immediate cause of death!

Fenimore had barely recovered from the impact of this discovery when the phone rang. He picked up, not waiting for Doyle.

"I hear you're a friend of the celebrated Ashburn family," Rafferty said.

"In a matter of speaking. Why?"

"In a matter of speaking," he mimicked Fenimore, "the medical examiner has labeled it a suspicious death and sent me the autopsy report."

So it was out.

"I was going to go back to the ME for a translation of this gobbledygook," Rafferty said, "but thought I'd check it out with you first."

"His initial collapse was thought to be an SCD episode. His father was diagnosed with an SCD tendency, and the condition is often genetic," Fenimore said.

"So what was he doing rowing?"

"That's a long story."

"Give me the short version."

Fenimore told him about Caroline Ashburn's request for help with her son; Chuck's subsequent examination by Dr. Burton; the doctor's report that he was SCD-free; the later discovery that he did, in fact, have an SCD tendency and had received an ICD implant. (He skipped adroitly over how this knowledge had come to light.)

"And he was still rowing?"

"Yes. He and his father hid his condition from his mother."

"Nice family. Go on."

"The kid was twenty-one, so legally he could do what he wanted. I tried to change his mind—but failed."

"Right."

"Now, the autopsy reveals"—Fenimore continued—"that Chuck had no evidence of cardiac dysfunction: no enlargement of the heart; no thickening of the arteries; and no apparent need for the ICD implant. The doctor's report was a fabrication and the implant was an unnecessary procedure."

"What the hell? Have you asked the father—*your pal*—about all this?"

"We're not on speaking terms at the moment."

"What about the doctor? Why would he falsify his reports?"

"I don't know. But I mean to find out."

"Fine. What about the lab report."

"I'm coming to that. The autopsy revealed an incredibly high potassium level. The low potassium that he registered upon admission to the CCU had to be corrected, but the replacement is always done gradually. I've never seen this degree of hypercorrection. It indicates that the potassium was given to Chuck all at once and could have been the cause of death."

"How did they give it to him?" Rafferty asked.

"Intravenously."

"Could someone have made a mistake?"

"Unlikely. It was too gross."

"That narrows the time down, at least. The lethal dose had to be administered after he was in the CCU," said Rafferty.

"That's right."

"It also eliminates a lot of people. Only medical personnel would know how to administer potassium via an IV."

"True—unless they paid someone to do it."

"You have a Machiavellian mind, Fenimore," the policeman said. "But why would someone want to kill the kid? Do you have any ideas?"

"No." Fenimore wasn't ready to share his PPI list just yet. "But I'm going to check out a few alibis."

"Be careful, Fenimore. Someone tried to drown you, remember?"

"This time, I promise I'll stick to dry land." He hung up.

Mrs. Doyle stood in the doorway, looking displeased. "It's that woman," she said in a low voice. "She's in the waiting room. She was going to just walk in on you, but I stopped her. She doesn't have an appointment. I was half tempted to throw her out."

Fenimore had often thought his nurse had missed her calling. She would have made a good bouncer. "What woman?"

"The Ashburn woman. I know, I know, she's suffered a terrible loss. But she's so pushy!"

"Easy does it," the doctor soothed. "Send her in."

Mrs. Doyle flounced out. At least as much as someone of her girth *could* flounce. A moment later, Caroline Ashburn came in. She did not look pushy. She looked weak and frail. His nurse must have been basing her opinion on past experience. Fenimore guided her to a chair.

As soon as she was seated, she said, in a voice that had lost most of its timbre, "I'm so sorry about your accident, Andrew." Fenimore could scarcely hear her. "I wanted to come to the hospital, but . . ."

"Nonsense. I'm sorry I couldn't get to the service." Liar. That had been the one silver lining in his hospital stay; he had been spared the ordeal of Chuck's funeral. But he could have bitten off his tongue, because the mention of the service triggered a choking sob from Caroline. He jumped up and offered his handkerchief. He always kept a clean, cotton one in his upper left jacket pocket, just in case.

She blew her nose noisily.

Fenimore pretended to study some papers on his desk until she regained her composure.

"I just wanted you to know that I appreciate all you tried to do, and . . ." She faltered. Fenimore was afraid she was going to break down again. But she took a deep breath and continued. "And I . . . I . . ." She looked around the office as if wondering where she was and how she got there.

"Are you all right, Caroline?"

"Oh yes . . . I just . . ." Again, she paused and the vacant stare returned.

Was this all caused by grief or could she possibly be taking something? "Has your doctor prescribed a sedative for you?" Fenimore asked.

"Hmm?"

"Tranquilizers. Are you taking them?"

She looked as if she had never heard of them.

"Caroline?"

She focused on him, but it seemed to require a great effort.

"How did you get here?"

"Uh . . . train."

"The Paoli Local?"

She nodded.

"And then you took a cab here?"

She nodded again.

"Just to thank me?"

Another nod.

"I appreciate your coming down," he said. "How is Charlie doing?"

She closed her eyes and shook her head mutely.

"I'm going to drive you home."

"Oh no." She was suddenly alert. "You have to limit your activity."

Ignoring this, he looked down at the paper on his desk. "But before we go, I want to tell you about Chuck's lab report—"

"No!" With a sudden burst of energy, she stood up. "I don't want to hear about it."

"But . . ." Fenimore rose too.

"I'm glad you've recovered." She produced a grim replica of a smile. "We'd better be going."

As Fenimore escorted her through the office, he told his nurse, a trifle defiantly, "I'm driving Mrs. Ashburn home."

She sent him a disapproving look.

CHAPTER 32

When Fenimore returned to his office, it was blessedly empty, except for Sal, who deigned to drop from the windowsill and wrap herself around his ankles. This unusual gesture conveyed the message that she had been worried about him. He reached down and scratched between her ears, to reassure her. If only humans could communicate so easily.

The phone rang.

"Hi, Fenimore."

A voice—vaguely familiar.

"Burton here. Heard about your accident. Bad luck."

Fenimore frowned at the phone. Luck had absolutely nothing to do with it.

"I had an idea. How about coming up to my place for a few days to recupe? I know we've just met, but I feel we're compatible. We both respect the old medical values. And, hey, we're brothers!" he said, referring to their membership in the same fraternity. "If you have a significant other, bring her along too."

Fenimore hated that term.

"It's nice up here this time of year. You'll recover a lot quicker if you get your lungs out of that smog factory."

"Nice of you to think of it, Burton, but I'm way behind, and—"

"Why don't you run it by your girlfriend? Maybe she'll change your mind."

Girlfriend. Another term he disliked.

"I have a hunting lodge in the woods, not far from my place. Very cozy and private. Charlie and I go there every fall."

Fenimore was getting irritated. "Thanks. Maybe some other time."

"Well okay, Fenimore."

Fenimore hung up. *And why do you falsify your reports and recommend unnecessary operations, Burton?* he thought savagely.

He had barely finished this thought when the phone rang again. This time it was Myra Henderson. Fenimore thanked her for the flowers she had sent him at the hospital. A beautiful arrangement of lilacs—lavender, pink, and white. When he had finished, she shocked him with the words "Maybe we should let the boathouses go."

"What?" Fenimore thought he had misheard her.

"If rowing is such a dangerous sport, maybe it should be outlawed."

"It's not the sport that's dangerous, it's the people," Fenimore objected hotly.

"I suppose. But a tragedy like that of the Ashburn boy, and your near drowning, makes one think. Puts everything in perspective. What is losing a few old buildings compared to losing lives?"

Had he been right about Myra? Did she want to get rid of the boathouses? "But we have to go on," he heard himself utter the banal refrain.

"That's what people always say." She sighed. "But no one has ever given me a good reason."

For the first time, Myra's voice sounded old and weary to Fenimore. He felt compelled to cheer her up. "How would you like to meet me for a martini tomorrow at one of your Bryn Mawr watering holes?"

"Do you mean it, Doctor?" She instantly revived.

"Of course."

"Then let's do it right and I'll come into town. We'll go to the Barchester." The Barchester was one of Philadelphia's most elegant residential hotels, located on Rittenhouse Square. Mrs. Henderson had lived there for forty years before a hip operation had forced her into a retirement home in the suburbs. "I've been put out to pasture, Doctor," she told him mournfully. "It will be a treat to get back to the city."

It seemed to Fenimore that she got back to the city fairly frequently—the regatta, the hearing at City Hall. "But that's a trip for you," he said, envisioning the elderly woman staggering onto the Paoli Local after two martinis.

"Pish posh. I still have Charles, you know. Not Charlie Ashburn—Charles, my chauffeur."

"In that case, it's a deal," Fenimore said. "What time?"

"Five o'clock, of course—the cocktail hour."

"I'll be there."

Plenty of phone calls—*all except the one I wanted*, Fenimore thought. Jennifer hadn't called to welcome him home. Where was she? Off in South Jersey picking cranberries with her Indian chief? That morose Montezuma!

"Doctor!" A voice roused him from his gloomy musings. It came from the kitchen. He followed it.

Doyle, Rat, and Tanya were seated cozily around the kitchen table having dinner.

"Hey, Doc. Have a seat." Horatio pointed to the remaining empty chair and a place set with a plate of spaghetti and sauce, tossed salad, garlic bread, and a Coke.

"It's about time." Mrs. Doyle rolled her eyes. "I called you."

"Sorry." He told her he'd been tied up on the phone. He sat down and dug in, without a single thought about cholesterol. After satisfying his appetite, he turned to Tanya. "How are you feeling?"

"Good." Her smile sparkled.

She certainly looked better. He challenged Mrs. Doyle. "What are you doing here?"

135

"Meet your new live-in cook, maid, and baby-sitter," she said cheerfully.

Since Jennifer seemed temporarily unavailable for any of these roles, Fenimore gave her a grateful smile.

"And you?" He turned to Horatio.

He shrugged.

"He keeps me company," Tanya said sweetly.

The boy flushed.

"Horatio has a surprise for you, Doctor," said Mrs. Doyle.

He looked at Rat. The boy bent and rolled up his cargo pant leg to his knee, exposing a pale, thin, naked calf.

"It's gone!"

Horatio smiled. "Yep! Came off today."

"This calls for a celebration! What have we got for dessert, Mrs. Doyle?"

"That's all taken care of." She nodded to Tanya.

The girl jumped up and ran to the refrigerator. Beaming, she came back bearing a huge chocolate cake decorated with a pink stick figure of Rat waving his cast in the air. "I made it myself," she said shyly.

Predictably, Horatio—the man of few words—said, "Cool."

Later that evening—after Horatio had gone home, Mrs. Doyle had gone to bed and Tanya was watching a favorite TV show—Fenimore pulled out his PPI list and studied it. This time he checked each person on the list for their medical expertise.

Henry Walsh: Hadn't Charlie told him that Hank's father had started out at medical school and then switched to law school? You could learn enough in the first year to master an IV line.

Hank Walsh: He was going to go to medical school, "and finish what my father started," he had told Jennifer. He was taking a year out to give Henley a try. With his interest in medicine, he had probably learned enough from reading and occasional visits to friends in the hospital to handle a simple IV.

136

Frank O'Brien: Every coach had to take courses in CPR and advanced life support. Surely he had a working knowledge of IVs.

William Ott: He had designed a number of hospitals and probably absorbed enough knowledge through osmosis to do a simple injection into an IV line.

Charlie was a surgeon, of course, and Caroline Ashburn had plenty of opportunity to absorb knowledge from her husband. And, it wouldn't be hard to look up the lethal dose of potassium in Charlie's *Physicians' Desk Reference.*

Jack Newborn: *No medical connections that I know of.* But he had plenty of dough to hire someone who did.

Myra Henderson: She had been a hospital patient often enough to observe how IV lines worked. And with her acute intelligence, she'd have no problem putting her knowledge to work.

Geoffrey Hunter-Powell: I know nothing about him. I'll have to look into his background.

Fenimore had just begun another list, headed "Alibis" when the phone interrupted him

"Hi."

Jennifer.

"Well, it's about time!" Fenimore said.

"Did you miss me?"

(Not "How are you feeling?" or "I'm so sorry, I was kidnapped and they taped my mouth shut.") "I suppose . . ."

"Good. How are you feeling?"

(Better late than never.) "Okay." He attempted a feeble tone.

"I have so much to tell you." They had not really talked since his accident because there were always two or three others in the room during visiting hours at the hospital. "Roaring Wings was wonderful. He's a fount of information. My book will throw a whole new light on the Native American." She bubbled over with enthusiasm.

"You actually got him to talk?"

"Oh yes. No problem. Once you touch what is closest to his heart . . ."

(He has a heart?)

". . . the history of the Lenape people—the stories just flow from him."

"Hmm." Fenimore called up a picture of the stoic, monosyllabic Lenape chief he knew and found Jennifer's description hard to swallow.

"And he made me a bona fide Lenape dinner!"

"Cracked corn and muskrat pie?"

"Don't be silly. Fresh catfish from the river and the most delicious corn bread you ever tasted."

Fenimore felt an alarm go off inside him. "Well, I'm glad you've finished your research. Now you can start writing."

"Oh, no. I've barely begun my research. I've scheduled another interview next weekend."

Fenimore was silent.

"Sorry for running on so," Jennifer misinterpreted his silence. "I should have asked about the Ashburns. Have there been any new developments?"

"Caroline was here."

"How is she?"

"About as you'd expect. But there was an aspect to her grief that worried me."

"Oh?"

"She seemed distracted, in a daze. Non compos mentis. I wondered if she was taking something."

"Tranquilizers?"

"I asked her that, but she was very vague. Her whole manner was disturbing."

"Well, I'm sure you'll figure it out. I have to run and finish typing my notes before I forget everything."

"He didn't go for the tape recorder, then?"

"No way. He almost threw me out when he saw it. But I convinced him to let me stay." She gave a conspiratorial giggle that Fenimore found disconcerting.

After she hung up, Fenimore stared at the phone for a long time. While he was still staring, it rang again. He picked up.

"Yo, Doc." Rafferty. "You're not holding out on me, are you?"

"What do you mean?" Fenimore's guilty conscience kicked in.

"This Ashburn case is heating up. I need all the information I can get."

"What do you want to know?"

"Let's get together tomorrow at my office and I'll pick your brains—say, eleven o'clock?"

"All right," Fenimore agreed reluctantly.

The case must be hot if Raff was willing to work on Sunday. Fenimore sighed. Suddenly he felt very tired. Almost too tired to climb the stairs to bed. He was half dozing in his chair, when he heard a noise. He looked up. Tanya was in the doorway.

"I was worried about you." She smiled.

"You were?"

"Uh-huh. Rat told me how sick you were, and . . ."

"Nice of you to worry," he said gruffly. "How is your cough?" He retreated into his physician role.

"Better. I wanna thank—"

"None of that. We're all happy to help you, Tanya. I'm glad Rat found you."

"Me too," she murmured.

"If you're tired of TV, there's a library full of books in there."

"Yeah, I saw them."

"Do you like to read?"

"Not much. I mean, I don't read much except for school."

"Let me show you." He led her back to the library. His hand automatically reached for the little green book, *Robinson Crusoe.* "Try that."

She held the little book a moment before opening it.

"You two may have something in common."

She gave him a quizzical look.

"Well, Crusoe was stranded on an island—and you were stranded in a cellar."

She curled up on the sofa with the book.

"But don't stay up too late," he warned, "It's important that you get your sleep."

She didn't answer; she was reading.

As Fenimore made his way slowly up the stairs, he wondered if he was missing something, not having a family.

CHAPTER 33

The next morning, Fenimore was awakened by chest pain. But the pain wasn't acute and it didn't radiate down his arm. Just a dull ache. The doctor in the ICU had warned him that near-drowning victims sometimes suffered symptoms days, even weeks after the event.

"Oh hell," he groaned. Accustomed to perfect health, he found any illness—even a common cold—exasperating. He reached for the phone, then remembered it was Sunday. He hated to disturb a doctor on Sunday. He decided to wait it out.

He was suddenly aware of unfamiliar noises floating up the stairwell. "What the . . . ?" He shoved his feet into his old slippers and shuffled out into the hall. Peering over the bannister, he saw an unusual sight. Mrs. Doyle and two teenagers playing cards at her desk. It was a game of slapjack and it had grown quite rough.

Whack! Rat slammed his hand on top of Tanya's hand, which had just landed on a fat pile of cards topped by a Jack.

"Ouch!" she squealed. "They're mine." She threw his hand off and grabbed up all the cards.

Mrs. Doyle sat benignly by, waiting her turn.

"Erumph." Fenimore cleared his throat. Three pairs of eyes turned upward.

"Oh, Doctor, we're—" Doyle stopped in mid-sentence and lunged to her feet. One look at Fenimore and her keen nurse's eye told her he was not well. She hurried to the bottom of the stairs. "Go back to bed. I'll be right up," she ordered. Turning to the young people she said, "Take your game into the other room."

They quickly folded their cards and disappeared.

Unlike Fenimore, Mrs. Doyle had no qualms about disturbing a doctor on Sunday. Once she had tucked Fenimore safely back in his bed, she dialed the home of Dr. Randolph Larkin, chief of cardiology at Fenimore's hospital. The doctor prescribed two aspirin and said he'd be right over. Although house calls were a thing of the past, when a colleague was sick, exceptions were made.

Twenty minutes later, Dr. Larkin rang the bell. Dressed for a lazy Sunday at home, he wore jeans, a sport shirt and Nikes. The fact that he had not taken time to change alarmed Mrs. Doyle. That probably meant it was urgent. She ushered him upstairs. As she mounted the stairs behind him, she caught a glimpse of Horatio and Tanya peering out of the library, their expressions anxious.

"Sorry to drag you out," Fenimore whispered. The chest pains had increased and his voice was weak.

"You can cover for me for the next six weeks, Fenimore," Larkin chuckled, as he took his stethoscope from his back hip pocket. Some of the old-school doctors still carried one with them all the time out of habit. "Did you take your aspirin like a good boy?"

Fenimore nodded. It was becoming an effort to talk.

After listening to Fenimore's chest for a moment, Larkin straightened up. "I think we'd better admit you, Andrew. You'll get better care at the hospital where there's a good staff and state-of-the-art equipment."

Too weak to protest, Fenimore closed his eyes.

Taking this as consent, Doyle ordered an ambulance. In the hall, after muttering several Hail Marys, she asked the doctor, "Is he bad?"

Larkin looked uneasy. "These near-drowning cases are hard to evaluate. This could be a minor episode, but we have to keep an eye on him. Can you accompany him to the hospital?"

Doyle thought fast. What about the children? Then she decided: If Rat had taken care of Tanya for all those weeks in the cellar, he should be able to look after her for a few hours here. She nodded.

A half-hour later, Fenimore was admitted to the ICU for the second time in a week.

CHAPTER 34

Jennifer was trying to decipher the notes she had taken from Roaring Wings. She wished her handwriting were more legible. She knew she should have typed them the minute she got home, while they were still fresh in her mind, instead of waiting a week.

The phone.

She put the notes aside and answered it.

Mrs. Doyle.

Andrew was in the ICU again. She slammed down the receiver and hurried out to hail a cab.

Horatio was restless. Doyle had told him to stay and look after Tanya, but he wanted to know how the doctor was doing. They were playing gin rummy, but his mind kept wandering and Tanya had won two games in a row.

"Pay attention, Rat," she said with a triumphant look as she won the third game.

"I'm tired," Rat said, laying down his cards. "Let's watch TV."

"You just don't like getting beat," Tanya grumbled. But she reached for the remote.

The ICU physician watched Fenimore's cardiogram on the monitor. Normal for three leads, then that disconcerting T wave. She took Fenimore's pulse. Slow but strong. She replaced his hand on the sheet. The fingers were long and slender, like an artist's or a musician's. She knew about Fenimore. Not only an exceptional cardiologist, but he had an excellent reputation as an amateur detective. She hoped he would wake up soon so she could talk to him about his cases—his criminal cases, that is.

Mrs. Doyle sat in the visitor's lounge at the end of the hall, leafing through a year-old copy of *People*. *Who were all these people?* she wondered. *Had they really been famous a year ago?* She threw the magazine down and began to pace. She shared the lounge with two other occupants—a skinny woman and a blubbery man. Jack Sprat and his wife, in reverse. What would she do if anything happened to the doctor? She refused to think about it. He had a strong constitution. He was going to be *fine*. She decided to look for a pay phone and check on the children.

Rafferty paced his office. It was eleven thirty. Where was Fenimore? Did he forget? Or was he deliberately avoiding him? He reached for the phone and dialed.

"Doctor's office," a young male voice answered.

"That you, Rat?"

"Yeah."

"Where is Doyle?"

"At the hospital with the doc."

"Helping him with a case?"

"No. She's helping *him*."

"What?"

"The doc took sick this morning and he's in the hospital again."

"Well, why didn't you say so?"

"I was gonna. . . ."

Rafferty hung up and grabbed his jacket from the back of his chair.

Mrs. Henderson had been sitting in the cocktail lounge of the Barchester Hotel for fifteen minutes, and she was not amused. She was unaccustomed to being kept waiting, and Dr. Fenimore was usually so prompt. Could she have mistaken the time? She glanced at her watch for the hundredth time. Her nieces and nephews told her she was getting forgetful, but she noticed that they often forgot things too. It wasn't a matter of age, it was a matter of overload. *We're all doing too many things these days,* she thought.

She tapped her fingers on the glass tabletop and played with the slim, elegant matchbook with "Barchester" printed in a silvery blue. For once, she blessed Philadelphia for its backward ways. They still allowed smoking in some of the more elite cocktail lounges. She took a cigarillo from her handbag and signaled the waiter. After he lit it for her, she ordered a martini, straight up, with an olive. If she had to wait, she might as well enjoy herself.

CHAPTER 35

It wasn't clear whose idea it was, but after Fenimore's friends had paid their respects at the ICU, they gathered, by common consent, back at his home office to determine who had caused the doctor's present deplorable condition.

When they arrived, Mrs. Doyle discovered a string of telephone messages from Mrs. Henderson, becoming more and more incoherent as they progressed. (Horatio had stopped answering after the third phone call.) The number left on the tape turned out to be the cell phone of her chauffeur. When Mrs. Doyle spoke to him, he said he would bring her around right away. Doyle wasn't sure whether "bring her around" referred to her geographical location or her physical condition.

Someone made the decision to order enough Chinese food to last the night, and they settled into the living room wearing expressions of grim determination. Rafferty ran the meeting and Doyle took notes (her hand was clearer than Jennifer's), while Jennifer, Horatio, and Mrs. Henderson, looked on—the latter consuming cups of black coffee at a rapid rate. Tanya sat in a corner absorbed in reading a little green book.

"First," said Rafferty, "does anyone know the doctor's latest thoughts on the Ashburn case?"

Silence.

"We could look through his desk. He often makes notes," said Jennifer.

Doyle disapproved of this invasion of the doctor's privacy at first, but, convinced by the others of the urgency of the situation, she finally agreed. She went into his inner office and came back with three sheets of paper. One was mysteriously headed PPIS, another read MEDICAL EXPERTISE, and the third bore the title ALIBIS, but was blank below. Rafferty scanned the first two sheets. Noting that Mrs. Henderson's name appeared under both headings, he decided not to pass the sheets around. He read the first list aloud, discreetly omitting the elderly woman's name. After her third cup of coffee, she appeared on the verge of sobriety. By the time Rafferty reached Jack Newborn, she said brightly, "Wouldn't it save time if you just passed the sheet around?"

"Er . . . I thought . . . if I read . . ." Rafferty fumbled.

"Nonsense. Let me have it." She reached out and grabbed the first sheet. "What does 'PPI' mean?"

Rafferty cleared his throat. "I don't know what the initials stand for, but judging from the names on the list, I think it refers to—er—possible suspects."

"That can't be," she said adamantly, "because *my* name's on the list."

Silence.

To everyone's surprise, Mrs. Henderson burst into hearty laughter. "Why that old buzzard!" she said. "Wait 'til I get my hands on him."

The meeting moved on. After everyone had read the PPI list and digested the motives Fenimore had jotted next to each name, Rafferty passed around the Medical Expertise list.

"Well, he's wrong there," Mrs. Henderson chuckled. "I haven't the slightest idea how an IV works."

When Rafferty came to the Alibis list, he held it up to show the group. "As you can see, the doctor hadn't gotten very far with this. But we discussed it, and I know what he was looking for. Since Chuck was murdered by a large dose of potassium injected into his IV line, the crime must have been committed after Chuck was admitted to the CCU. What we need to find out is where all the PPIs were between the time Chuck was admitted and when he died. To be specific, between one-thirty and three-thirty that afternoon."

"I was chairing a meeting of the Historical Society at Twelfth and Locust," Mrs. Henderson spoke up, a mischievous glint in her eye. "And I have thirty witnesses to prove it."

"That's a relief," said Rafferty. "I was feeling a little nervous with a possible killer in the room."

General laughter relieved the tension.

Turning serious again, Rafferty said, "How are we going to find out the rest?"

"Can't you just ask them for their alibis?" said Jennifer.

"I could," Rafferty said, "but I'd rather not get their wind up just yet. The killer is more likely to show his or her hand if they think we don't suspect them."

"I could do it."

Everyone turned to look at Horatio, who had been silent until now.

"I could just hang around the boathouse and keep my ears open. I'd just be a dumb kid askin' stupid questions 'cause I wanna learn how to row. Nobody'd suspect me."

Rafferty looked thoughtful. Then he said, "When can you start?"

"Tomorrow—right after school."

Shortly after this decision was made, the party broke up. Everyone seemed satisfied, except Tanya. Toward the end of the meeting, she had finished her book and heard Rat volunteer for something. She sensed that it might be dangerous. Before Horatio left, she whispered in his ear, "Be careful, Rat."

"Sure." He planted a kiss on her nose.

149

Later, when Tanya was helping Mrs. Doyle clear away the remains of the Chinese food, she noticed that Horatio's fortune cookie was still intact. She broke it open and pulled out the slip of paper. "Look before you leap," the message read.

Unaware of the plans being made in his very own living room, Fenimore dozed fitfully in the ICU. He was dimly aware of figures flitting to and fro on rubber-soled shoes, the hum of medical equipment, and whispered consultations. Dr. Larkin had dropped by once, right after Fenimore had been admitted, but that was long ago. No one had paid much attention to him since. That was probably a good sign. Too much attention in the ICU was usually not a good thing. He wondered how Doyle was coping with her teenage charges, whether Jennifer would come see him tomorrow, and if Rat was behaving himself. His last thought, before he dozed off, was: *I hope no one tampers with my IV!*

Rafferty had had the same thought in the middle of the meeting. Not wanting to alarm the others, he had kept it to himself. As soon as he got outside, he dialed headquarters on his cell and ordered a twenty-four-hour police guard outside the ICU.

CHAPTER 36

Horatio knew nothing about boats. He didn't even know how to swim. A Philadelphia ghetto doesn't provide much opportunity for learning either of these things. But he had plenty of questions.

As he trotted along Kelly Drive, dodging cyclists, joggers, and Rollerbladers, he wondered how those skinny little boats stayed above water. What were they made of? And how fast could they go? Spying a shabby sign that said ROWBOATS FOR HIRE, he left the path and headed down to the river's edge. The dock was a shoddy patchwork of weathered wood, but the rowboats looked sturdy enough. If he took his time and stuck close to the shore he should be okay. He approached the man dozing on a rickety chair, and coughed.

"Wha—?"

"I wanna rent a boat."

The man looked him over. "Ever rowed before?"

"Sure."

"Uh-huh."

"Look, man. I've got money." Horatio showed him the brand-new ten-dollar bill Mrs. Doyle had given him from petty cash.

"You have to sign a slip." The man reached in his pocket and pulled out a crumpled printed form, which, when signed, would release him from all responsibility for injuries (such as drowning, etc.). Horatio signed. The man pocketed the new ten and gave Horatio an old five. As an afterthought, he reached into a bin behind his chair and handed the boy a faded orange pillow with straps attached to it.

"What's that?" the boy asked.

"Ain't you ever seen one?"

"Oh sure," the boy said quickly. He grabbed it and tossed it into the boat.

When Horatio climbed into the boat, it rocked violently. Seating himself cautiously, he carefully placed the oars in the locks on each side.

"Watch out for the falls," were the man's parting words. But he neglected to mention in which direction the falls were—up or downriver.

Horatio edged his new vehicle gingerly along the shore. His destination was not far. He could see the Windsor Club dock about one hundred yards ahead, where two young men were sliding a boat into the water. His plan was to ease up to the dock and pretend to be a dumb city kid. *Pretend?* He laughed out loud, scaring a duck—*or was it a goose?*—from the water. He would come every day after school until they got used to seeing him hanging around. Pretty soon they wouldn't take any notice of him and he could ask as many questions and eavesdrop as much as he wanted.

He caught on to the rowing quickly. He was strong and the boat slipped easily through the water. He liked knowing he was causing it. He also liked the feel of the sun on his back and the breeze ruffling his hair. *This is cool,* he thought, and suddenly wished Tanya were with him.

By the time he reached the Windsor dock, the two rowers had left. The only person in sight was some phony-looking dude in plaid shorts, a T-shirt with some fancy gold picture on the pocket, and sandals which probably cost a grand apiece.

"Hi ho!" The dude greeted him with a lethargic wave and sidled over to the edge of the dock.

"Hi."

"What's your name, mate?"

Mate? "Rat."

"Of course." A knowing smile crept over his thin lips. "That's why you're 'messing about in boats'." He chortled, referring to that other Rat in *Wind in the Willows.*

"Huh?"

He shrugged. "A literary allusion."

"Uh-huh." *What a pain in the ass,* thought Horatio. *But he might know something.* "What's your name?"

"Looking somewhat affronted, he finally drawled in his funny accent, "Geoffrey Hunter-Powell."

"A mouthful," Horatio muttered. But the name rang a bell. It was on the two lists the doctor had made. This must be that British scout from Henley. He was glad he'd paid attention during the meeting last night.

"Are you a rower?" Rat asked.

"Sculler."

"Whatever."

"Occasionally. But I don't compete."

"Why not?"

He shrugged.

"It looks like fun," Rat said.

"If you enjoy working up a sweat," he said.

"Did you know Chuck?"

"Chuck?"

"The guy that died?"

"Oh—a bit."

"Did you visit him at the hospital?"

"Whatever for?" His surprise seemed genuine.

"To see how he was." *Slimebag,* Horatio thought.

"No. He was only an acquaintance, you know."

Horatio wanted to puke but restrained himself. He was doing this for the doctor, he reminded himself, and kept his cool.

"Hey, Geoff! Who's your friend?" An African American rower joined them. With a friendly grin he leaned down and shook Rat's hand.

"His name's 'Rat,'" said the slimebag. "He likes 'messing about in boats.'" He gave the newcomer a sly grin.

The newcomer ignored him. "You thinking about becoming a rower?" he asked Horatio.

Horatio flushed. "Maybe."

"You can take lessons, you know."

"Yeah?"

"They have some brochures in the boathouse. I'll get you one."

Geoffrey, looking bored, moved away.

When the black rower returned with the brochure, he said. "I'm Hank. Anytime you have any questions, let me know."

"Gee, thanks."

Horatio glanced at his watch and was surprised to see that his hour was almost up. He had to return the boat. As he rowed off he thought, *I talked to two suspects. Not bad for the first day.*

CHAPTER 37

Rafferty called Horatio at home that night and demanded a full account of his progress. The boy reported that the British dude hadn't gone to the hospital to see Chuck and seemed bored with the whole thing. And Hank Walsh was a nice guy.

"How did you get to the boathouse?"

"By boat."

"Can you swim."

"No."

"For God's sake, Rat, did you wear a life jacket?"

"Huh?"

"It's a puffy vest, usually orange, with buckles and straps."

"Oh, that. I thought it was a pillow. I sat on it."

Rafferty groaned. "Listen, next time you set foot in a boat you wear that pillow."

"Okay, okay."

After the policeman calmed down, he said in a quieter tone, "You did well, Rat. Keep up the good work."

The next day it rained. Not a gentle patter but a torrential downpour. Horatio stayed in the office, and when he had finished his work he played a raucous game of Monopoly with Tanya. He taught her how to steal money from the bank and hide it under the table, and then objected hotly when she tried to rob him.

Mrs. Doyle decided to order pizza for dinner. She was too tired to cook. Besides, she was worried. When she called the ICU that evening, the report was "No change." While the teenagers had a friendly fight over the last piece of pizza, the nurse tried to immerse herself in a romance novel. Somehow Lady Bottomly and Lord Topperfield's lovelife failed to hold her attention.

The following day, the sun was shining. When Doyle called the ICU, she was told the doctor had a good night and would probably be moved to a private room the next day. Exhilarated, the nurse pounded out twenty Medicare forms on the word processor and agreed to watch *Oprah* with Tanya. She had to renege on the latter, however, because the show's guests were unsuitable. They were all young women who had been abused by their fathers. Doyle grabbed the remote, and, to Tanya's disgust, changed the channel. They watched an old black-and-white movie starring Clark Gable and Carole Lombard. Mrs. Doyle was in ecstasy, while Tanya played solitaire and prayed that Horatio would show up soon. But, of course, he didn't, because the sun was out and he was down on the river.

As Horatio made his way to the boat rental, he passed a man on the riverbank who was using some kind of weird equipment. Always curious, the boy stopped and asked, "Whatcha doin'?"

"Surveying," came the curt reply.

Not easily put off, Horatio asked, "Surveying what?"

"The riverbank. We're planning to put a marina here—once we get rid of those old boathouses."

Horatio's interest quickened. Glancing around, he spied the man's briefcase, leaning against a tree. On it, engraved in gold, was the name—W. Ott—one of the names on the doctor's lists.

Turning back to the man, he said, "Hey, that's cool. Are you the guy who's gonna build it?"

"I'm the principal architect," he said pompously.

"Is it true they're gonna be video games and a skateboard rink?"

Warming to the boy's enthusiasm, Ott said, "I believe those are included in the plans."

"Wow! When will it happen?"

"Not for some time, I'm afraid. These things aren't accomplished overnight." He frowned. "Unfortunately, there are a few obstacles in our way. For example, those ugly eyesores must come down." With a sweep of his hand, he gestured at Boathouse Row.

"Huh, that shouldn't be hard. One stick of dynamite and *poof*!" Horatio laughed.

The architect looked at Horatio with renewed interest.

"Besides, that rowing thing is dangerous. Didn't some guy drop dead here a week ago?" Horatio asked. "And didn't some old guy almost drown?"

"Now that you mention it, there was a rowing accident here. They took the fellow to HUP and he died in the CCU."

"Were you there?" Horatio feigned a look of grisly curiosity.

"No, but I work nearby, at the Architecture School." Tiring of Horatio's company, he began to fiddle with his equipment again.

Taking the hint, the boy ambled away. He had found out what he wanted to know.

It was Horatio's lucky day. When he arrived at the boathouse, dutifully wearing a faded orange life jacket, Frank O'Brien was on the dock instructing some new recruits in the basic steps of rowing. Trying to look as inconspicuous as possible, the boy sat in his battered rowboat, well out of the way. As the young men, looking strong and fit, listened intently to their coach, Horatio tried to think of some way to get his attention. He had an idea. He would stage a minor accident. The coach's back was to him and the students' attention was fixed on their teacher. Horatio ducked down low and began to slowly rock the boat. Unfortunately, despite its age (or perhaps because of it), it was sturdily built and didn't tip easily. Giving up, Horatio slipped over the side and began splashing and yelling for help. To make his plight seem more realistic, he had removed the life jacket. He also let go of the side of the boat. Suddenly, he realized he *really* did need help. Despite his flailing arms and churning feet, he was sinking and the water was closing over his head!

The next thing Horatio knew, he was lying flat on his back, staring at a few puffy clouds in a blue sky and O'Brien's face was a few inches from his own.

"You okay?" the coach asked.

Horatio looked from the blue sky into the coach's eyes, which were almost as blue. "Uh-huh," he said. He shook the water from his hair and tried to sit up.

"Take it easy," the coach said, and gave him a hand.

The new recruits were all standing around, gaping at him. He felt like an idiot. "Sorry," Horatio mumbled. "I guess I slipped."

"Can't you swim?" O'Brien asked.

He shook his head.

He turned to his recruits. "Which of you guys wants to teach this guy to swim?"

The wanna-be rowers looked at one another, each hoping someone else would volunteer. Then Hank appeared.

"Hey," he said when he saw Horatio. "That's the kid that was here the other day."

Horatio held his breath, wondering what he would do if they suspected him of spying.

"He wants to row," Hank said.

"Well he better learn how to swim first," the coach grumbled. "He almost drowned." But he eyed Horatio in a new way, evaluating his physique from head to foot.

"Shit, man. What's the matter with you?" Hank said to the boy.

Horatio looked down at the water, wanting to jump in again.

Hank came closer. "Listen. You come back tomorrow and I'll teach you to swim. And you come on foot. No more boats, until I tell you." He stepped into Horatio's rowboat. "I'll take this back, Coach," he said. "You leave this kid to me."

The recruits looked relieved. The coach ordered them to bring down a shell while he showed Horatio out.

O'Brien led Horatio through the rows of bays, where the shells were stored on racks, and up a short flight of wooden stairs into the boathouse. There was a living room, with chairs, a sofa, a fireplace—even a bar and a TV. Over the mantel hung framed photos of past rowing teams who had won awards. When the coach saw Horatio looking at one picture, he said, "Those fellas won the Diamond Sculls last year—one of the highest rowing awards."

"Wow!" Horatio stared intently. "Wasn't that the race the guy who died was going for?"

O'Brien's expression turned somber. "You're really up on the rowing scene, aren't you, kid?" He looked at the boy carefully.

"Yeah." Horatio said. "I follow all the regattas. Were you here when Ashburn died?"

"Chuck didn't die here," he said quietly. "He died later, at the hospital. And, yes, I was there." He passed a hand across his face, as if to wipe away the image. "Come on, I have to get back to my class." He hurried Horatio to a wooden door, the upper half of which was made of colored glass.

Horatio thought the whole place was kind of pretty. Not an eyesore at all.

"When you come for your swimming lesson," O'Brien said, "come to this door and press the buzzer. Someone will let you in."

"Thanks, man. And I'm sorry about . . ."

"Forget it." He grinned. "You learn to swim and who knows? Someday you may be a rower."

As Horatio walked down the path to Kelly Drive, he was

overwhelmed by a confusing mix of emotions: humiliated over his fake drowning prank; proud that he had gained some useful information for Rafferty; and exhilarated at the thought that someday he might become a rower.

CHAPTER 38

For the second time in a week, Fenimore awoke to find himself in a hospital bed. He looked around the bare room. Friends couldn't be expected to send flowers twice in one week. Before moving he lay still, checking out various functions. No chest pain. His breathing was normal. He could see the crack in the ceiling; his eyes were okay. He could hear the murmur of traffic, punctuated by horns outside the window; his ears were intact. The smell of bacon and scrambled eggs reached him from the tray next to his bed. (How come they smelled so good and tasted so awful?) His nose was still working. He wriggled his fingers and toes. They all moved smoothly enough. What was he doing here?

Dr. Larkin appeared in the doorway. "Say, Fenimore, you're looking chipper."

"When can I leave?"

"Not so fast." He came over to the bed. "You just left the ICU. We have to watch you, old boy."

"I have work to do."

"It can wait. We have your hospital patients covered, and I know you have a capable office manager."

Fenimore smiled at this understatement. But his concerns

weren't for his medical practice. They were for the Ashburn case. Every minute he lay in the hospital, the case was growing colder.

Larkin listened to Fenimore's chest, asked him to say "Ah," and felt his neck and abdomen for stray nodes. When he was done, Fenimore asked again, "Seriously, how long will I be in here?"

"Two to three days, I should say. We don't want to risk another relapse. If I were you, I'd take a few weeks off. Take a trip. Go to the shore or the mountains. A near-drowning episode is no joke, Andy—especially at your age."

"I'm only forty-three."

"That's when we start to go downhill."

"Speak for yourself," Fenimore muttered to his physician's retreating back.

Fenimore passed the morning consuming watery scrambled eggs, limp bacon, and tepid coffee; being prodded, poked, and interrogated by various unidentified people; and answering phone calls from concerned friends. Mrs. Doyle was first. After inquiring about his health, she assured him that Tanya was fine. She had a good appetite. "She put up a good fight with Horatio over the last piece of pizza last night."

Jennifer was next. Her voice sounded faint and far away. She was heading for South Jersey and using her cell phone. "I'll have to make it short because my battery's running low," she said.

Rafferty sounded brisk and cheerful, but when Fenimore asked him about the Ashburn case, he sensed the policeman was holding something back.

Rat was the last to call. Fenimore was touched to learn that the boy had skipped recess to call from a public pay phone. "Hey, man, when are they lettin' you out?"

"Two or three days."

"Well, don't worry. I've got the office under control." (No mention of Mrs. Doyle.)

"That's great, Rat."

"Yeah. And I'll have some news for you pretty soon."

"News?"

"I've been covering the waterfront."

"What?"

"You'll see. I left some stuff on your desk. Uh . . . there's the bell . . . gotta go!" Click.

Fenimore was musing over his last call when an aide came in bearing a potted plant with a tall stem and huge, glossy leaves, but no flowers.

"There's no card," the aide said.

Fenimore rooted in the soil with his finger for a plastic tag that would identify the plant, to no avail. He didn't need one, however. He recognized the plant right away. *Oleander*. And he was also familiar with its deadly qualities.

CHAPTER 39

Fenimore was released the next morning amid many dire warnings from Dr. Larkin. The first thing he saw when he returned home, was the pile of "stuff" Horatio had left on his desk. The top sheet bore a diagram rendered in Rat's large, ungainly hand, labeled ALIBIS (SATURDAY/1:30 P.M. to 3:30 P.M.). The diagram showed the whereabouts of all the suspects at the time of Chuck's death.

Fenimore called Rafferty. "Did you see this timetable of Rat's?"

"Yeah, he faxed me a copy. Nice job. He's a bright kid."

"Did you check out these alibis?"

"Yeah, I called the Planning Commission. They were holding a meeting during that time."

"That eliminates Wormwood, Newborn, and Grub." Fenimore hated to relinquish Grub. She seemed such a likely candidate. "Are you sure there were no absentees?"

"I checked that out."

"What about Henderson?"

"You mean you haven't heard from her?"

"No. Why should I?"

"She found out she was on your suspect list."

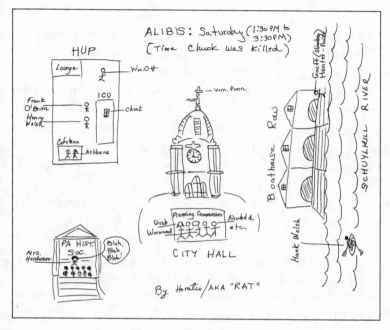

HORATIO'S DIAGRAM

"Oh my God."

"She took it pretty well, but I'd check out any unmarked packages in the mail, if I were you."

That explained the oleander. Myra's sense of humor always had a touch of the macabre.

"She's in the clear," Rafferty went on. "I called the Historical Society and learned she was chairing a meeting of thirty members that afternoon, just like she said."

"That leaves just three suspects: O'Brien, Ott, and Walsh Sr."

"If you discount the parents . . ."

"I saw Ott roaming the campus at HUP that afternoon, and O'Brien and Walsh were hanging around the CCU."

"All three had motives, but Ott's was the strongest," said Rafferty. "His whole career hangs on that marina, I'll bet."

"But which of the three would know how to handle an IV?"

"And how would they get ahold of potassium?"

They were silent for a minute, pondering these questions.

Finally Fenimore said, "Where do we go from here?"

"To lunch," said Rafferty and hung up.

Fenimore glanced at his watch. Sure enough, it was after twelve. He didn't feel hungry. He decided to take a walk—the only exercise his doctor allowed him. But before he could get out of the office, the phone rang. Dan Burton, offering his hunting lodge for the weekend—again. "It's a great place to recuperate, Fenimore. Quiet, scenic. Bring your girlfriend."

Fenimore told him he was much too busy to take time off right now.

"All work and no play makes Fenimore a dull boy," Burton said. "If you change your mind, just give me a ding-a-ling. . . ."

Ding-a-ling? Fenimore felt a wave of nausea. As he replaced the receiver, he pondered Burton's motive for badgering him to come to the Poconos. He barely knew the man.

It was a lovely day, and as Fenimore strolled down Pine Street he relished his liberation from the hospital and was happy to be alive. He breathed in the sweet scent of the linden trees and gazed benevolently on the sidewalk cafés overflowing with young people. He paused. *And not so young people.* He had spied a familiar face. He could never forget the strong, handsome features of the last Lenape chief. But what was he doing in the city which he professed to abhor? And why was he smiling? Roaring Wings never smiled. Seeking the cause for these two minor miracles, he glanced at the Indian's companion. A shock ran through him.

Jennifer was talking animatedly while Roaring Wings listened intently with that serene smile on his face.

Fenimore looked around for some way to escape, but Jennifer had spotted him and beckoned. As Fenimore came toward their table, he saw that her color was high and she was flustered.

"You know Andrew Fenimore," she said to Roaring Wings.

"Of course." The chief rose and shook hands. "Won't you join us?" he said politely.

"No, thanks. I'm just out for a stroll. Doctor's orders," Fenimore said.

"How are you feeling?" asked Jennifer.

"Much better, thank you. How is your book coming?" He was appalled by their formality.

Jennifer glanced at Roaring Wings, who answered for her. "She's doing a fine job. I read the first chapter last night. Just the right tone." Again he smiled.

Excusing himself, Fenimore left them.

When Fenimore arrived home, he still had no appetite. His mood was low and his thoughts confused. Maybe it was part of his convalescence. He knew that such a traumatic experience often had aftershocks. The mind and body don't always heal simultaneously. Sometimes one lagged behind the other. His main thought was to get Jen out of town, away from Roaring Wings. Another thought intruded. Burton's second invitation. Why was he so insistent? Could it have something to do with Chuck's death? After all, he did falsify the boy's records. Suddenly he had an idea. Why not kill two birds with one stone? Get Jen out of town and learn more about Burton. He reached for the phone and punched in Burton's number.

CHAPTER 40

Once on the road, Fenimore had mixed feelings about the trip to the Poconos. He had no business taking a weekend off. He was backed up with work as a result of his two hospitalizations. He felt guilty about sticking Mrs. Doyle with Tanya for a whole weekend. Jennifer had accepted his invitation readily enough, so his fears about her and Roaring Wings were probably groundless. And he should be working on the Ashburn case. (Although, in a way, he was. Burton fit into it somehow. He was sure of it. He just wasn't sure where.) His suspicions about his host had increased in direct proportion to the urgency of his invitation to come to his place. What if Burton was not merely a sleazy doctor who committed fraud (or "wrongdoing" as the media euphemistically calls it)? What if Burton was actually dangerous? By accepting his invitation he might be putting Jen in jeopardy. Take it easy, Fenimore. You're overreacting—a symptom of your illness. Burton is probably just a good Samaritan—or simply a lonely bachelor seeking companionship.

"The covered bridge should be coming up soon." Jennifer held the map in one hand as she gazed through the windshield.

"It better be. It's getting dark," Fenimore said.

"There it is!" Jennifer pointed at a peaked roof ahead. "According to the map, Burton's place is only a few miles from here."

As the car rumbled over the wooden bridge, Fenimore wondered when the bridge was built and whether it was up to its job. To his relief, they made it to the other side. "Now what?"

Jennifer squinted at the map in the waning light. "We go three miles, then make a right at Fox Creek Lane. It looks like the lane ends at the lake—and his house."

"Thank God. I'm starved," Fenimore said.

"Didn't you say he was a gourmet cook?"

"That's what he told me."

"Let's hope he's going to practice his skills on us."

Fox Creek Lane was a narrow, winding road lined with thick pine trees. Fenimore shut off the air conditioning and rolled down the windows. (His old Chevy still had windows with handles.) The fresh scent of pine filled the car.

"Umm." Jennifer inhaled deeply.

Although their scent was pleasant, the pines hemmed the car in on both sides making Fenimore claustrophobic. They also darkened the road, forcing him to turn on his headlights. Twisting and turning through the tunnel of foliage, Fenmore was glad when they glimpsed the lake ahead, shimmering under the last rays of the sun.

Burton's home was a sprawling, stone house surrounded by a wide screened porch overlooking the lake. Knowing their host was a bachelor, Fenimore wondered why he needed such a big spread. As they drove up, the doctor came out on the porch—a ghostly figure in the twilight. He must have been looking for them. He greeted them enthusiastically, seated them in comfortable wicker chairs, and told them to enjoy the view while he rustled up something to drink. The view consisted of a black body of water surrounded by more pine trees. The sinking sun cut a golden path across the dark surface. Fenimore glanced at Jennifer. She looked relaxed and content. "Maybe this wasn't such a bad idea," he said.

She smiled. "Every now and then it's good to get away. You gain perspective."

Fenimore wondered if she was referring to him or to herself. She came over and kissed the top of his head. He grabbed her hand, pulled her down on his lap, and kissed her.

"Whew!" she came up for air.

Fenimore didn't let her breathe too long.

"Well . . ." Burton stood before them, bearing a tray of gin and tonics and an array of hors d'oeuvres that would have been more appropriate at a wedding reception than in such a rustic retreat. "I see the mountain air has worked its magic already," he said.

Jennifer blushed and went back to her chair.

Over drinks, Burton answered Fenimore's unasked question—why he needed so much space.

"My hobby is woodcarving. I need room to store my materials and also to display my finished products. I'll show you my sculpture after dinner."

They talked about the area. How developers and conservationists were at sword's point. (So what's new?) They all unanimously sided with the conservationists. "In the old days it was the loggers we wanted to get rid of," Burton said. "Now it's the developers."

"Do you use local wood for your sculpture?" Jennifer asked.

"Not anymore. I import wood from all over the world—from Africa, Malaysia, South America. The wood around here is too inferior for my work."

Dinner, a culinary delight, was served on the porch. Poached salmon, fresh asparagus, and crème brûlée—accompanied by some very good wines. Small candles scattered along the porch railing provided the only illumination, and they soon guttered out. In the deepening dark, Fenimore's companions receded, becoming disembodied voices.

After dessert, a chilly breeze sprang up from the lake and Burton steered them inside for the liqueurs. The living room was vast. The stone walls soared to a ceiling filled with smoke-blackened beams and a fire flickered in a cavernous fireplace. But it wasn't the beams or the fireplace that drew the guests' attention. It was the animals—all life-size and native to the area—captured in wood. A deer caught on the verge of leaping over a stream; a bear rearing up from the underbrush; rabbits, raccoons, beavers, wood-chucks, and birds—all the carvings rendered in poses so natural it was hard to believe they weren't alive. The room had been trans-formed into a wooded glen.

"You're very talented," Jennifer said, sipping her crème de menthe. "Where did you study?"

"The Pine Lake Conservatory," Burton said, a sly glint in his eye.

"You mean you're self-taught?" Fenimore said.

He nodded. "I've played with native woods since I was a boy. Later, when I could afford it, I imported more exotic types." He stroked the sorrel neck of the deer. "This is from Tanganyika," he said. He moved over to the bear. "And this mahogany is from the forests of Brazil." He knelt beside a hare. "And the wood for this little fellow came from Hawaii."

"Amazing," said Fenimore.

"You see, choosing the perfect wood to match your subject is an art in itself. Making the right choice can determine whether your work is mediocre or a masterpiece."

"Do you exhibit your work?" Jennifer asked.

"Occasionally."

"In Philadelphia?"

He winced. "No. New York, London, Paris."

Fenimore was suddenly struck by the doctor's metamorphosis from the boring, hail-fellow-well-met Burton had portrayed in his office, to the distinguished artist he was presenting tonight. *How many personalities did this man have tucked away?* he won-dered. But Fenimore shouldn't have been too surprised. He knew some doctors wore a protective mask with their patients, prefer-ring to keep their private lives to themselves. He had never felt the need to do that.

Beneath the smell of wood smoke and the lingering aroma of their gourmet dinner, Jennifer detected another, less appealing odor. She couldn't quite put her finger on it. Then it hit her. Zoo! Like the distinctive smell of nursing homes, you can't completely hide the smell of live animals in captivity.

"How do you sculpt your subjects?" Jennifer asked demurely. "From photographs?"

Burton hesitated, then said, "No. I sculpt from life."

"In the woods?" asked Fenimore. "That must be a problem. How do you get them to stand still?"

He smiled. "Would you like to see?"

His guests nodded. Burton led Fenimore and Jennifer through the rambling house. On the threshold to the kitchen, they paused. Furnished with two state-of-the-art stoves, a walk-in refrigerator, a massive freezer, and all the latest culinary apparatus, it was every chef's dream. The center of the room was dominated by a thick wooden table that had been meticulously polished to show off its fine grain. To Jennifer, it looked like a chopping block—for a giant.

When they finished admiring the kitchen, Burton ushered them through a door into a large cinder-block room resembling a garage. But there were no cars in evidence, and the odor of animals, not automobiles, permeated the air. The walls were lined with cages, varying in size and strength. Only one cage was occupied by a small gray lump with a pink hairless tail. Jennifer identified a possum. The largest of the cages had heavy steel bars and could have easily housed the live model for the mahogany bear in the living room.

Fennimore reached out and shook the cage. It remained rooted. "Sturdy enough," he said with wonder.

"But is it humane?" Jennifer couldn't help blurting.

Burton's eyebrows shot up. "I treat my animals very well. A sick or dead animal is of no use to me," he said dryly. "And their confinement is only temporary." He reached into the possum's cage and chucked it under the chin. The small mammal remained motionless. "Why even Beatrix Potter, the famous children's author, kept her mice and rabbits confined in her room while she sketched them."

Confined, but not caged, Jennifer thought. On their return trip through the kitchen, she eyed the chopping block apprehensively. What a perfect place to dismember a rabbit or a deer before preparing it for a gourmet meal—after it has served its artistic purpose.

Back in the living room, the fire had dwindled to a few red coals, and in the semi-darkness the sculpted animals cast outsized shadows on the walls. The aura of a pleasant wooded glen had been replaced by the more sinister feel of the forest in *Hansel and Gretel* or *Snow White*. Fenimore and Jennifer felt heavily drowsy. The result of good food, wine, fire, and mountain air, Fenimore diagnosed.

"It's getting late," Burton, the perfect host, said. "I'll take you to the lodge. It's only a short walk from here."

Collecting their overnight bags, the small party made its way down the path, through the woods. The exercise roused the guests and they became aware of their surroundings. There was no moon and the darkness crowded in on them like thick cloth. The only illumination was the slender ray from Burton's flashlight. The dense darkness seemed to smother sound as well as sight. There was no murmur of birds, no buzz of insects, or shuffle of beasts. Everyone seemed to have been anesthetized for the night.

The lodge was completely dark when they entered. "No electricity," Burton said, "or running water," he added, as if these were points in its favor. But it had its own stone fireplace and all the necessary ingredients for building a fire had been provided—newspaper, kindling, and logs. Burton, an expert woodsman, assembled them quickly with the aid of his flashlight. "It gets cold in the mountains at night," he said, "even in the summer." Striking a match, he held it under the kindling until it flared.

"You'll find more blankets in the closet," he said, dusting off his hands, "and if you need anything else, I'm just up the path."

Fenimore wondered how he would be able to find his way "up the path" without a flashlight. But before he could ask for one, the door had closed. He and Jennifer were alone with the glow of the fire. Fenimore took Jennifer in his arms and held her close. After a minute, to his dismay, she said, "I'm falling asleep on my feet."

"Shall I make some coffee?" he asked hopefully, forgetting about the lack of water.

With a drowsy smile, she said, "I'd need a whole pot to keep me awake tonight. It must be that mountain air."

Fenimore felt unusually tired himself. A few minutes later they were both sleeping soundly under the patchwork quilt.

CHAPTER 41

Fenimore wasn't sure what woke him. The fire had died. The cabin was pitch black—and cold. He sat up. There was something else. His eyes smarted and he began to cough. *Smoke?* He reached out for Jennifer.

"What's up?" Waking at his touch, she too began to cough.

"I think there's a fire somewhere."

Jennifer sniffed. "My God!"

Fenimore slipped out of bed and felt his way to the door. "It's locked," he said.

"Well, unlock it."

"I can't see."

Jennifer stumbled over her own shoes as she made for the fireplace. "Do you know where he put the matches?"

"No." Fenimore broke into a spasm of coughing. When he recovered, he said, "I think you're supposed to keep low. Smoke rises."

Ignoring this advice, Jennifer felt for the matches on the rough mantel. No luck. She searched the hearth. "I can't believe I'm looking for matches in the middle of a fire!" What began as a laugh ended in a paroxysm of coughing.

"Come over to the door," Fenimore ordered.

Giving up on the matches, she crawled toward him.

"Lie down and put your face against the base. There's a crack. I can feel the draft."

She did as she was told. "But we have to get out," she muttered, her mouth against the crack. "What about the lock?"

"I think it's locked from the outside."

"What?"

"Did you see a window when we came in?"

"Yes. Above the bed. But it's too small for us to climb through."

"We could break the glass and at least get some air," Fenimore gasped. "And maybe if we yell, Burton will hear us." He crawled back to the bed, piled the pillows up, and stood on top of them. Now he could reach the window, but when he tried to raise it, it wouldn't budge. Back on the floor, he felt for his shoes. Finding one, he again climbed up, coughing the whole time. He hit the window with the heel. Unlike in the movies, the glass did not break at the first blow. He tried again. Nothing.

"That would work better with a foot in it," Jennifer croaked.

"What?"

"Wait a minute." On hands and knees, Jennifer crossed the floor to the other side of the bed, fumbled for one of her clogs, shoved it on, and climbed onto the bed next to Fenimore.

"What're you doing?"

"Can you lift me?" she asked.

"Sure, but . . ." He grabbed her around the waist and raised her a little.

"Higher." When her feet were level with the lowest windowpane, she cried, "Watch out!" and kicked with all her strength.

There was a sharp crack, followed by the sound of falling glass.

"Nice save!" Fenimore cried, almost dropping the star goalie in his excitement. They pushed their faces up to the small opening and inhaled the feeble trickle of cold air that filtered through. "Let's yell," Fenimore said. "Maybe Burton will hear us."

Fenimore's yell was husky; the smoke had made him hoarse. Jennifer tried to yell too, but her voice was almost gone. The chances of Burton hearing them while he slept were next to zero. *If only I could locate the source of the smoke,* Fenimore thought. There didn't seem to be any flames. And he felt no heat. The smoke was thicker near the fireplace. Maybe the fire was contained in the chimney. But even if he found the fire, he had no way to put it out. There was no running water, Burton had stated proudly. "To hell with rustic living!" Fenimore said in Jennifer's ear, trying to keep her spirits up.

She didn't answer.

"Jen?"

No response.

With a shock, he realized the only reason she was still standing was because he was holding her.

Bang! bang! bang! "Fenimore! Are you in there? Open up!"

Slowly Fenimore recognized the voice. Not Burton. Charlie Ashburn.

He shook Jennifer, but she remained inert. Fortunately she weighed little. He carried her down from the bed and over to the door. He croaked to Charlie, "It's locked from the outside."

"Christ!"

A few seconds later he heard a key scrape in the lock and the door flew open.

Fenimore staggered out with Jennifer in his arms.

"Let me have her," Charlie said.

Fenimore insisted on carrying her himself.

"Come on." Charlie guided them through the woods with his flashlight.

"Where's Burton?" Fenimore asked after taking gulps of the cold fresh air.

"I don't know. He wasn't home and I smelled smoke. I followed the smell to the lodge. I have a key because Burton and I come here to hunt every fall."

When they reached the house, Burton was just pulling up in his Land Rover. He jumped out. "What's going on?"

Charlie told him.

"My God!" He looked stricken. "I must have locked the door on the outside out of habit. My God," he repeated, staring at Jennifer.

At that moment she opened her eyes and began to cough.

"The cold air must have brought her around." Burton's relief was palpable.

"Let me down," she said grumpily.

"Are you sure?" Fenimore asked.

She nodded.

He let her down, but kept his arm around her.

"Better call the fire department," Charlie told Burton, "if you want to save the lodge."

They all went inside while Burton made the call. Fenimore grabbed a throw from the sofa and wrapped it around Jennifer, who was shivering. It wasn't until they were seated and sipping straight whiskey from paper cups that anyone thought to ask Charlie why he was there.

"It's Caroline. She's asking for you, Fenimore." He revealed that he had called Mrs. Doyle, waking her in the middle of the night, to locate him. When he didn't get an answer he decided to drive up.

For the first time, Fenimore looked carefully at Charlie, and was struck by how much he had aged since he had last seen him.

"She tried to take her own life tonight," he said.

Fenimore studied his old classmate and his former animosity dissolved. "How?"

"Pills. She keeps saying she has to talk to you. That's why I'm here."

"Well, what's holding us up?" Fenimore stood.

Burton came back from his call.

"We have to go," Charlie said. "I'm sure your volunteers will soon have everything under control. I'll help you rebuild the lodge, if it comes to that."

"Sure, but don't you want to stay? I have plenty of room."

"No," Fenimore said quickly, "but thanks for your hospitality." He wasn't being sarcastic. He was muttering banalities because he was too exhausted to do anything else.

Looking bewildered, Burton walked them to their cars. Jennifer, still clasping the throw around her, started to peel it off.

"Keep it. Please." Burton thrust it back at her and helped her into the car.

Charlie backed up his Chrysler, turned it around, and took the lead. Fenimore followed in his Chevy. The two cars sped toward Philadelphia.

CHAPTER 42

While Fenimore drove, Jennifer slept. He wasn't sleepy anymore. As soon as he began to drive he woke up. His mind was sharp, and he was beginning to see things clearly for the first time. Why had he agreed to visit Burton? He had sensed there was something phony about his invitation from the beginning. Partly to get Jennifer out of town, but also to find out more about Burton. And he *had* learned more about the doctor. He had a luxurious spread, more than most country doctors could afford, and he indulged his fine tastes in food, wine, and travel. Not to mention his expensive wood carving hobby. Then there was that private zoo he maintained.

There's no crime in any of that, Fenimore.

Unless you acquire the means for this affluent life illegally, he answered himself, *by doing unnecessary medical procedures, for example.*

He would like Jennifer's opinion. He glanced over at her. Head tilted back, the moonlight flickering across her face, a faint smile on her lips, she looked so vulnerable. He couldn't bring himself to disturb her. She had been through a lot and needed to rest.

What if Charlie hadn't come? He gripped the steering wheel. That didn't bear thinking about. Why had the door been locked from the outside? Was that really an accident? None of this would have happened if Rafferty hadn't planted that seed of doubt in his mind. Suggesting that Jennifer might be getting tired of him!

With a sigh, Jennifer turned her face away from him, toward the window.

The entrance to the Northeast Extension loomed ahead. Following Charlie, he eased into the E-ZPass lane. Once on the turnpike, his thoughts returned to Burton. He went over his contacts with him, from their first meeting—when he had gone to see him for a checkup. The doctor had seemed competent and professional. He had taken his time, but he hadn't dawdled, supplying the right amount of innocuous small talk. Fenimore had been the one in the wrong. He had come under false pretenses—and he had rifled the doctor's files. But the knowledge he had uncovered had soured his opinion of Burton. What kind of hanky-panky was he involved in? Why had he diagnosed Chuck as an SCD candidate when there were no clinical signs he had such a condition? Had he based his diagnosis on a mere genetic possibility? Because Chuck's father was SCD prone? To recommend an ICD implant on such flimsy evidence was highly unorthodox. Then, to hide the truth from Chuck's mother . . .

At the Valley Forge interchange, Fenimore passed a lumbering oil truck to keep on Charlie's tail. When he caught up with the Chrysler, his thoughts flipped back to Burton. When had he last seen him?

At that cardiology meeting at HUP—the day Chuck collapsed. He had spotted Burton at the back of the room. Knowing he was Chuck's doctor and an old friend of the Ashburns, he had gone over—against his better judgment—and told him about the boy. He had seemed genuinely upset, and he had planned to go to the CCU after the lecture to look at Chuck's lab tests. But the lecture had been long, and when it was over Burton had decided he had to get home. Fenimore had thought it a little odd at the time. . . . And when Fenimore had returned to the CCU, he had found Chuck had died.

181

A screech of brakes behind him. In his rearview mirror, Fenimore saw an angry trucker shaking his fist and cursing. Jennifer woke up briefly and immediately fell back to sleep.

Fenimore had slowed down, to the consternation of the trucker, because he had a new thought. A disturbing one. Could Burton have left the lecture—and come back later?

Why not? The lights were out. He was sitting in the back. He could have slipped out and gone to the CCU. The lecture had gone on for over an hour, plenty of time for Burton to find a white coat, a syringe, and some potassium. Doctors were always moving in and out of the CCU. No one paid any attention. For someone who knew what he was doing, it would take only a few seconds to inject something into an IV line. Then all he had to do was drop the syringe into a trash can, stash the coat in a closet or rest room, and hightail it back to the lecture. It would be tight, but it could be done. A vivid picture of Burton came back to Fenimore: standing up, giving a big yawn, relaying his opinion of the lecture.

Could he have yawned *after* killing Chuck?

It had never occurred to Fenimore to suspect Burton, because he had the perfect alibi. He was at the lecture with *him*! His mind moved with lightning speed now, jumping from one conclusion to another. What about the masked man—his own attacker? Could that have been Burton too? But why would Burton want to kill him? Could he have found out I'd been into his files? His nurse seemed suspicious. But how would he have known I planned to go rowing that day?

Because you told him, jackass!

With horror, Fenimore remembered casually mentioning that a row on the river might clear his head. *The goldfish was rapidly turning into a shark!*

Once again a horn blasted behind him. He speeded up, focusing on the car in front. A black Honda had replaced Charlie's black Chrysler. He'd lost him. So what? They were going to the same place. He'd catch up with him at the hospital.

Reminded of his destination, Fenimore's thoughts switched from Burton to Caroline. Why had she attempted suicide? Because of Chuck's death alone? Or was there something more?

"Where are we?" Jennifer asked groggily.

"The Schuylkill Expressway." He looked at her tenderly. "Are you okay?"

"As well as can be expected, after being almost murdered."

"Murdered?" He had come to the same conclusion, but had wanted to protect Jennifer from the knowledge.

Jennifer stared at him. "Don't tell me you thought that was an accident?"

"Well . . ."

"Give me a break."

"How did you come to that conclusion?"

"Instinct. I didn't like him from the start. Such ego! All that stuff about exhibiting in London and Paris. And the choice of wood making the difference between mediocrity and a master-piece. Oh *please*."

"Lots of people have big egos, but they aren't murderers."

"True, but most murderers have big egos. Whatever gets in their way, they get rid of. Zap!"

"Why did he want to get rid of us?"

"You. I just happened to be along. You must be a big threat to him. Do you know something about him that could hurt him if it came out?"

Fenimore frowned.

"Something that might damage his career?"

"Burton must have known I would find out that Chuck didn't need an ICD implant and that he, as the boy's family physician, had recommended it. There was no evidence of any SCD tendency in the boy's echocardiograms or his autopsy. If this came out, he could lose his license," Fenimore said, "and he could never practice again."

"Bingo!"

"So he locked the door on purpose, set the fire, and—"

"And . . . if we weren't burned to a crisp, there was always the chopping block."

"Chopping block?"

"Never mind." Jennifer shuddered.

CHAPTER 43

Dawn was breaking over the skyline as the two cars entered the city. It was a rosy-fingered dawn, full of promise—completely out of sync with the moods of the people from Pine Lake. They were grateful for one thing, though. They had beat the rush-hour traffic. The streets of Philadelphia were deserted. They made their way quickly to the hospital and found street parking easily.

The daily bustle had not yet begun. The vast lobby was silent and empty, except for a stoic security guard standing near the entrance and a sleepy receptionist, sitting behind the information desk.

Jennifer said, "I'll wait in the lobby."

The two men headed for the elevators.

When they reached Caroline's room, Charlie went in first while Fenimore remained in the corridor. Charlie came out quickly. "She's awake," he said.

The only light in the room came through the window—from the sun's early rays. Caroline was propped up in bed, staring into space.

He moved to the end of the bed.

"Thank God," Caroline whispered.

He pulled up a chair to the bedside.

"I had to tell someone, and you're the only one who will understand." She looked past him, out the window. When she spoke, her words came in a rush. "I killed him, Andrew. I killed my own son."

"What are you talking about?"

"I pretended I wanted Chuck to go to Henley to throw you off the track. But all the time I had this plan."

Fenimore looked incredulous.

"It's true. I got it from Charlie's *PDR*. I found out that if I combined my diuretic with Charlie's prostate medicine, the mixture would cause low blood pressure, dizziness, even fainting—all symptoms that resemble SCD. I ground up two of my own water pills and mixed it with two capsules of Charlie's prostate medicine. Then, when I was making Chuck's lunch, I sprinkled the mixture in his sandwich. It was only supposed to make him dizzy—or pass out momentarily. I thought the symptoms would be mistaken for an SCD attack and stop him from rowing forever!" Her features became contorted into a grotesque mask. "But I'm no doctor, Andrew . . . and *I put in too much!*" She began to sob—great wrenching sobs.

"Stop it!" Fenimore grabbed Caroline and shook her.

She stared.

"You didn't kill Chuck."

"What . . . ?"

"Did you inject potassium into his IV line?"

Her eyes widened.

"Did you?" he hissed.

"No!" She shook her head. "What are you talking about?"

"That's how Chuck died. Someone injected a lethal dose of potassium into his IV line while he was unconscious in the CCU."

Caroline fainted.

CHAPTER 44

Leaving Caroline to the care of her nurses and Charlie, Fenimore went back to the lobby to tell Jennifer what had happened.

"Poor soul. I never liked her, but I wouldn't wish such a fate on anyone."

"I have to go to the CCU and check out a few things. Do you want to take the car?"

"No, I'll take the bus home. But . . . be careful." She gave him a quick peck on the cheek.

He was in luck. The nurse who had been in charge the day Chuck had died was on duty. He asked if he could speak to her privately when she had a minute. While he waited in the corridor, he went over the latest events. Everything was still conjecture. There was no proof that Burton had arranged that fire. And there was no witness to testify that he had injected potassium into Chuck's IV line. In fact, nothing had happened to eliminate the other two men from his PPI list—Ott and O'Brien. He needed one concrete piece of evidence. *Maybe this nurse could provide it,* he thought as she came toward him.

"What can I do for you, Doctor?" she asked.

"On the day Chuck Ashburn died, can you remember anyone coming into the CCU who didn't belong there?"

"Oh my." She sighed. "That's a tough one. It was almost a week ago, you know."

"I know," Fenimore said apologetically. "But it's very important."

She closed her eyes. Then she said slowly, "There was one orderly . . ."

"Yes?"

"He was only there for a minute 'to check the bedpans,' he said."

"What did he look like?" Fenimore prodded.

"Nondescript. Middle-height, middle-weight, middle-aged . . ." She brightened. "That's why I remember him. . . . He was middle-aged. Most orderlies are young guys. You know, working their way through college."

"Do you have a schedule of the orderlies assigned to the CCU?"

She nodded. "I'll get it."

Fenimore's pulse had quickened. Was he on to something?

The nurse came back with the sheet. Fenimore scanned it. "You've been very helpful, Ms. . . . ?"

"Rochester. I'm glad." She smiled, and returned to her demanding duties.

From the schedule, Fenimore had learned there were two orderlies on duty the day Chuck died—one from 7:00 A.M. to 4:00 P.M.; the other from 4:00 P.M. to 7:00 A.M. The orderly who was on duty during the time Chuck was in the CCU was Juan Roderigo. Fenimore tracked him down in the basement, where he was returning a gurney that had a squeaky wheel in need of repair. Juan looked about twenty and was anything but nondescript. Dark and solidly built, he was what the girls would call "a hunk," thought Fenimore. When he asked Juan why he was an orderly, he said, "To help pay my tuition at the community college."

"Are you planning to be a doctor?"

He laughed. "No way. A lawyer. But this was the only job I could get."

"Well, law and medicine are closely intertwined these days," Fenimore said with a touch of bitterness. He thanked the young man and left.

Now all he needed was a positive identification. He glanced at his watch. In a few hours the cardiology meeting would take place in the Hirst Auditorium, as it had a week ago Saturday. *If only Burton attends,* Fenimore thought. He decided to call the doctor's office and see if he could find out anything.

"May I speak to Dr. Burton?"

"I'm sorry, he's left for the day." The receptionist didn't sound very sorry.

"Did he go to Philadelphia?" He risked an impertinent question.

"I really couldn't say." Huffy, stuffy.

"Thanks." He hung up.

He decided to proceed on the assumption that Burton *would* attend.

Fenimore called Jennifer. "Could you have dinner with me tonight?"

"Sure."

"No trips to South Jersey?" He tried to sound nonchalant.

"Roaring Wings is at a powwow this weekend. He asked me to go, but I had to help Dad in the shop."

"I'll meet you at the Four Seasons at six."

"How posh!"

"Nothing but the best, my dear. By the way, there'll be another guest."

"Oh?"

"Burton."

"Oh!"

"Sorry, but there's method to my madness."

"Though this be madness, yet there is method in't," Jennifer corrected him.

"Well, yes, that too."

· · · ·

At ten minutes of two, Fenimore took a seat at the back of the Hirst Auditorium. Pretending to be engrossed in the latest *JAMA*, his heart beat a rapid tattoo in his chest. The hall was nearly filled and the head of the cardiology department was about to introduce the guest speaker. *Burton isn't coming*, Fenimore decided.

Someone slipped into the seat beside him. Fenimore looked up. Burton gave him a hesitant smile. *Still embarrassed about that fire*, Fenimore thought. He smiled back.

This time the lecture was actually on a topic of interest to Fenimore, and it was blissfully short. When it ended, he turned to Burton and took the plunge.

"I was hoping you'd be here. How would you like to join Jen and me for dinner tonight?" Before Burton could refuse, Fenimore, knowing his expensive tastes, added quickly, "We have a reservation at the Four Seasons and would be very pleased if you could join us. It's our way of saying we have no hard feelings about last night."

The doctor accepted eagerly.

"Fine. I have to stop by the CCU before we leave, but I won't be long."

On the way to the CCU, Fenimore asked about the lodge. "Was it badly damaged?"

"No. They caught it in time. It seems some damn bird built a nest in the chimney and blocked it up. I hired a chimney sweep to clean it out good and proper."

When they reached the CCU, Fenimore said, "I'll be right back." He ducked inside. He returned a minute later, followed by Ms. Rochester. The nurse glanced at Burton and continued down the corridor to the rest room.

Fenimore checked his watch. "We have a couple of hours to kill before dinner. How about a walk by the river?"

"Sounds good to me." Burton was in a fine mood, amenable to anything Fenimore suggested. Fenimore, on the other hand, was nervous and irritable. It was all he could do to hold up his end of the conversation. At the first phone booth they came to, he excused himself to Burton. "I have to check on a patient."

"You don't have a cell?" Burton was surprised.

"Left it home," Fenimore lied and pulled the door closed, leaving Burton outside. He dialed the CCU.

"Wachovia Bank."

He was so nervous he had dialed the wrong number. On the second try he got it right. He asked to speak to Ms. Rochester. When she came on the line, Fenimore identified himself and held his breath.

"That was the guy," she said. And there was no trace of doubt in her voice.

Fenimore's knees sagged. "Th . . . thanks," he stuttered.

After she hung up, he continued to hold the receiver, pretending to talk, giving himself time to recover. He stared at the back of the nondescript, middle-aged man, patiently waiting outside. He couldn't believe what he had just heard. Doctors were trained to save lives, not destroy them. How could he . . . ? Such a young man . . . ? Images of Chuck rose before him—in his shell, rowing toward the finish line; at his mother's dinner table, quiet and unobtrusive; seated next to him in the car, fiercely defending his philosophy: *"To be the best I can be!"*

Fenimore swallowed hard and squeezed the receiver as if it were a life support. *How could he sit across from this man and eat dinner?*

Burton glanced at the booth, wondering what was keeping him.

He could call Rafferty, of course. Tell him what he'd found out. But he wasn't sure he had enough evidence for a conviction. *What he needed was a confession.* Girding himself, Fenimore replaced the receiver and stepped out.

"No emergency, I hope?" Burton said.

"No. Everything's under control. Let's go for that walk."

The next two hours were the longest Fenimore had ever endured.

He had no memory of where they walked or what they talked about. As they walked, he periodically felt cold and then broke into a sweat. He would momentarily forget his newfound knowledge, only to suddenly remember, *I'm chatting with a killer!*

CHAPTER 45

Jennifer was waiting in the hotel lobby. Fenimore almost didn't recognize her. She was dressed in an elegant black silk sheath, accented with silver and turquoise jewelry. Burton was impressed too. He took her arm and, over cocktails, directed all his conversation to her. He didn't even notice when Fenimore excused himself to make a phone call. But Jennifer did. She cast him a wary look as he left.

He called Charlie. He wasn't sure how to break the news about Burton, but he had to find out what the doctor's motive was, and the only person who could help with that was Charlie. He was sure it had something to do with those false reports in Chuck's file.

"Charlie?"

"Andy." They were back on speaking terms, ever since Fenimore had come to Caroline's rescue.

"I'm sorry to bother you at dinnertime."

"I'm not eating much these days. I just came back from the hospital."

"How is Caroline?"

"Better. You helped her, Andy. She told me about the potassium."

His tone altered, becoming tense with suppressed anger. "Do you have any leads?"

"I'm afraid so."

"What?" The question was like a branch snapping.

"Not 'what.' Who."

"Who, then."

"Burton."

The line was deadly quiet. Finally, *"That can't be."*

"He posed as an orderly when Chuck was in the CCU. I got a positive identification from the head nurse this afternoon."

"She saw him do it?"

"No, but she saw him in the CCU, dressed like an orderly. He was 'checking bedpans,' he said."

Silence.

"Now I'm looking for a motive. I thought you might be able to help."

More silence.

"Charlie?"

When Charlie spoke, his voice was flat, completely without expression. "Dan Burton and I have been friends since college. He's our family doctor. We've gone hunting every fall since I can remember. He taught Chuck to hunt. . . ."

"I know, Charlie, but—"

"You're telling me he killed my son?"

"It looks that way."

"Where is he?"

"He's here with Jen and me. We're having dinner at the Four Seasons."

"You're what?"

"It's a long story. I had to trick him into going to the CCU with me so the nurse could identify him. The only way I could do that was to ask him for dinner."

"I'm coming down."

"No. Don't do that, Charlie. He's a cool customer. We don't want to get his wind up until we have all the evidence."

194

"I'm coming."

"But you won't get here in time for dinner, and—"

"I'll get there in time for dessert."

"Charlie—"

He hung up.

"You sure are conscientious," Burton said when Fenimore rejoined them. "You know," he turned to Jennifer, "this bozo has made half a dozen business calls since I've been with him. Is he always like this?"

"Pretty much." Jennifer smiled.

"When does he have time for you?"

"Oh, he manages to squeeze me in."

"Have you ordered?" Fenimore asked.

"Not yet," said Jen. "We were waiting for you."

"Well, I'm here." He signaled the waiter for menus. When he brought them, Fenimore mumbled, "Charlie may drop by later." He thought Burton blanched, but it was hard to tell in the candlelit room.

Fenimore survived dinner by making occasional monosyllabic comments. Jennifer carried the brunt of the conversation with Burton. Fenimore kept glancing surreptitiously under the table at his watch. He figured it would take Charlie about forty-five minutes to get from Bryn Mawr to town. Rush hour was nearly over and he was coming from the other direction.

Their entrées had been cleared away and they had just been issued dessert menus when Charlie breezed in the door.

Fenimore's appetite for dessert, which had been slight to begin with, vanished.

"So how come I wasn't invited?" Charlie slid into the remaining empty chair. "How're you doing, Burton?" He punched him playfully. "Keeping the boonies on their toes? What're you all drinking?" He caught the eye of the waiter. "How about some brandy?" He winked at Jennifer. "We should celebrate. It's not often Burton comes to town."

Jennifer sensed that Charlie was putting on an act. No man who had just lost his son, and almost lost his wife, would behave in such a jocular manner. She glanced at Fenimore.

Fenimore gave her a bland smile. He had begun to sweat again.

By nine o'clock, they had all switched to scotch, and, at Charlie's insistence, moved into the bar. The doctors exchanged doctor jokes, while Jennifer listened politely and laughed obediently. Fenimore knew she hated doctor jokes. Fenimore had to hand it to Charlie. He was putting on a good show.

By eleven everyone was quite drunk, except Fenimore. He had sipped slowly, deliberately rationing himself. He wanted to be sober, in case of an emergency.

But there was no emergency. At one point Charlie and Fenimore ended up in the men's room together. Fenimore took the opportunity to ask him again about Burton's motive. Feeling no pain, Charlie made a confession: Burton had been blackmailing him for years. "He threatened to tell Caroline about Chuck's cardiac condition if I didn't pay up," he said.

So that's how Burton paid for his spread in the Poconos; the exotic, imported woods; the fine food and wines. Of course, Charlie's part in all this wasn't exactly sterling. He decided not to disclose Burton's greater deception. The fact that Chuck had *not* suffered any SCD tendency. That he was perfectly healthy. Burton had lied about Chuck's condition so Charlie would continue to pay up.

"Why did you let Chuck row, Charlie, when you knew he was at risk?" Fenimore asked.

"*Let him?* Are you crazy? You've never had kids, have you, Fenimore?" He zipped up. "Chuck was of age. He did what he wanted. He wouldn't listen to me, or to anyone else."

Fenimore knew firsthand this was true. "Then why were you afraid of Caroline finding out?"

They were washing their hands.

"*I* wasn't. It was Chuck. He knew if his mother found out, she'd be nagging him to quit rowing every day of his life. He wouldn't have a moment's peace."

"What are you going to do?" Fenimore asked anxiously. He suddenly remembered the Mafia-like shove he had once received from Charlie.

"Relax, Fenimore. I'm a law-abiding citizen. You know the old adage, 'Two wrongs don't make a right.'" He patted his arm. "Shall we rejoin the party?"

To Fenimore's dismay, they had two more rounds of drinks, and then Charlie said, "Burton, you have to stay at my place tonight. You're much too drunk to drive to the Poconos."

"Awr no, I'm awr right." He rose clumsily to his feet.

"What about you, Charlie?" Fenimore said. "Maybe I'd better drive you both home."

"Nah, I'm fine." And, indeed, he seemed fine. Maybe he had been rationing himself, too.

"Well, *I* would like a ride home," Jennier said, still elegant, if slightly tipsy.

"I'll take care of you," Fenimore told her.

"Lucky boy." Burton gave her a lascivious look.

It took all Fenimore's restraint not to punch him.

Charlie left an enormous tip for the bartender, which he richly deserved, and they staggered out to the street.

"Swell party!" Charlie said, giving Fenimore and Jen each a bear hug. Burton was about to follow suit, but Charlie grabbed him and steered him toward the parking garage. The last Fenimore and Jennifer heard of the two doctors, they were singing some old college song—off-key.

When they reached the car, Jennifer asked, "What was that all about?"

"The old-school tie gone awry," Fenimore said grimly.

CHAPTER 46

Fenimore couldn't sleep. He was deeply worried and furious with himself for telling Charlie about Burton. He should have kept his mouth shut and gone straight to Rafferty. Poor judgment. What the hell was the matter with him?

He got up and paced the room. He tried to read, to no avail. Sal, registering her annoyance, moved into Tanya's room. He went downstairs to the kitchen and made some chamomile tea. It didn't help. Nothing helped. He went back to bed and lay, staring at the dark rectangle of his bedroom window. He watched it change from black, to charcoal, to gray. When it was pale gray, he got up and dressed.

His first thought was to call Rafferty, but it was Sunday, the only day his friend was free to be with his family. Instead, he called Charlie.

"Hey, Fenimore. That was some party. I needed that. It was like a good old-fashioned Irish wake—"

"You're comparing me to a corpse?"

"Well, you were a little stiff last night."

"How is Burton?" Fenimore asked, uneasily.

"Great. He's stuffing his face with ham and eggs, topped off with some hair of the dog—a Bloody Mary. Want to talk to him?"

"Yes."

As soon as Burton got on the phone, Fenimore said, "I'd like to drive your car out to you. That way you can leave for home right from Charlie's. It would save you a trip."

"That's damned nice of you, Fenimore—"

"What's damned nice?" Fenimore heard Charlie in the background.

"Wait a minute," Burton said, and Charlie came back on.

"We're going for a row this morning, Andy. Want to join us? Oh, that's right, you're off rowing for a while. You're on the wagon. Ha, ha, ha. Well, we'll miss you. . . ."

"Charlie, how many Bloody Marys have you had?"

"Now, Fenimore, none of your Calvinist sermons."

"I'm no Presbyterian."

"You act like one sometimes."

"I thought Burton only rowed rowboats," Fenimore said tensely.

"That's right. But I'm going to teach him the real thing today."

Fenimore heard Burton yell something in the background, but he couldn't make it out. He urgently repeated to Charlie his offer to drive Burton's car out to him. But Charlie squelched that. "We have other plans. Sorry you can't join us."

Before Fenimore could answer, Charlie hung up.

Fenimore called Rafferty and told the policeman his fears.

"What time do you estimate they'll get to the boathouse?" Rafferty asked.

Fenimore calculated how long it would take them to finish breakfast, then the trip from Bryn Mawr to Boathouse Row with traffic. "About an hour, give or take a few minutes."

"I'll be there."

He had barely hung up when Doyle, Rat, and Tanya piled into his bedroom and dragged him downstairs for a sumptuous breakfast of bacon, eggs, and waffles with fresh strawberries. But he was too anxious to eat. He swallowed only enough to satisfy the three cooks. Apparently, breakfast had been a group effort: Doyle had done the eggs, Rat, the bacon, and Tanya, the waffles. When they were finished, Doyle cleaned up and the teenagers tried to entice Fenimore into a game of gin rummy. But he said he was meeting some friends at the boathouse.

"Not rowing?" Doyle asked sharply.

"Heaven forbid," Fenimore assured her and hurried upstairs to dress.

CHAPTER 47

An ambulance and two police cars were parked in front of the boathouse. A cluster of curiosity seekers were trying to peer through the fence. A policeman was protecting the gate to the dock. Fenimore pushed his way through the rubberneckers.

"I'm a doctor—and a member of the club," he told the guard.

After Fenimore showed identification, the guard let him pass. He was approaching the dock at a run when he saw two medics lift Burton onto a gurney. Charlie and Rafferty were standing to one side, looking on. Fenimore watched as one medic pulled a blanket over Burton's face.

When Fenimore was sure his legs would carry him he went over to the two men.

Rafferty looked up. Charlie averted his gaze.

"An accident," Rafferty said.

Charlie shifted slightly.

The medics raised the gurney and moved away.

"What happened?" Fenimore finally managed to ask.

"We were out on the river," blurted Charlie, eager to talk. "Each in a single. I was shouting directions to Dan. And he was doing well. I looked away for a minute, starting to pull upriver, when I heard a yell. I turned to look and he had tipped. The shell was upside down and Burton was nowhere in sight. I told him about that string that releases the shoes, but . . . I guess he forgot."

Fenimore felt cold, remembering his own plunge.

"Anyway, I dove in and freed him, and managed to drag him onto the dock. Some young rowers were there, and gave him CPR. . . ." He faltered.

"Go on," Rafferty prodded.

"While they were working on him, I called 911. But by the time they got here, he . . . was gone."

"I came in while they were giving CPR," Rafferty said. "It seems you miscalculated, Fenimore. You forgot it was Sunday and traffic was light. They got here sooner than you expected."

Charlie looked bewildered. He thought Rafferty had come in answer to the 911 call. He began to shake.

"Someone get a blanket!" Fenimore shouted.

A young man disappeared into the boathouse and returned with a gray blanket. Fenimore threw it over Charlie's shoulders. "He's in shock," he told Rafferty. "He'd better come home with me."

The policeman nodded. "Take him home. I'll be in touch."

Back at the house, Fenimore took Charlie into his inner office. He sat him down and drew a dusty bottle of scotch from a drawer. He poured two shots into a tumbler and gave it to him. Charlie reached for it. He was shaking so badly he had to use both hands to get the glass to his mouth. Fenimore waited, letting the drink take effect. When Charlie stopped shaking, he asked him again, "What happened?"

Charlie repeated verbatim what he had said on the dock. This time he added, "Those kids rescued both shells."

They sat in silence for a while. Then Fenimore drove Charlie home.

• • •

Later that night, Fenimore lay awake, going over Charlie's story. Something nagged at him. Something was not quite right. The next morning, he rose early and went down to the boathouse. A bunch of young rowers were just returning from their early morning practice rows. Fenimore stopped them. "Were any of you fellows here yesterday during the accident?"

"I was." A young man stepped forward. "I helped with the CPR."

"So did I," spoke up another.

"Did you see who was in *The Zephyr*?" Fenimore asked.

The two youths who had spoken up looked puzzled. "No," said the first. "Both men were in the water by the time I saw them."

"Me too," said the second. "But no one's allowed to use *The Zephyr* except the Ashburns," he added.

Meaning Charlie must have been in The Zephyr . . . *Or was he?*

Fenimore went to the bay and scanned the oars. *The Zephyr Pair* were in their usual niche, a little separate from the regular oars. They were lighter, he remembered. Regular oars would be too heavy for the lighter craft—dangerous, even. He went outside and asked one of the rowers, "Do you know if the oars were lost yesterday?"

"Oh, yeah. We managed to save the shells, but not the oars. They slipped down river ahead of the boats and went over the falls."

"Lucky it wasn't the *Zephyr*'s," Fenimore said. "They'd be hard to replace."

"Yeah. They were custom-made."

Fenimore knew it would be difficult for an expert to row *The Zephyr* with ordinary oars, let alone a novice who was navigating a shell for the first time. Also, Burton was heavier than Chuck—by a good ten pounds. The extra weight might upset the balance. Of course, capsizing wouldn't have been the end of Burton. He could swim. *But he had been locked into those shoes!* And who knew how long it took Charlie to release him? There were no witnesses.

203

. . .

Fenimore walked up Kelly Drive, deep in thought. Absently he dodged cyclists, joggers, and strollers. "No one's allowed to use *The Zephyr* except the Ashburns." The boy's words echoed in his ears. He kept walking. The crowd on the path was growing, and he was having trouble avoiding a collision. He paused by the statue of Jack Kelly. The sculptor had captured the famous rower in the first step of the rowing cycle—the catch. The green-bronze figure gleamed in the sun, full of vigor and grace. That's what the sport was all about—grace under pressure. The old Hemingway maxim. But that had nothing to do with putting a novice in an especially light shell with a pair of too-heavy oars. The odds were unfairly stacked. He shouldn't have been in a singles shell the first time out anyway. Charlie should have taken him out in a double until he learned the ropes. Burton didn't have a chance.

Fenimore slowed down.

A jogger swerved around him.

Fenimore had slowed down because he again remembered Burton—after the cardiology lecture—feigning a yawn. *Right after he killed Chuck!*

He stood still.

"Watch it!" A cyclist narrowly missed him.

He started walking again, still thinking. *And shortly after the lecture, Burton must have gone down to the river, rented a motorboat, and tried to drown me!* Fenimore shivered.

But how did he know which boat I would choose? he asked himself.

That wouldn't be hard. Most of the rowers knew he always used *The Folly,* his father's old shell. All Burton would have had to do was ask someone.

So Burton had committed one murder, attempted another, and—for icing on the cake—there was the blackmail scheme. . . .

He stepped off the path and made his way to the river. Finding an empty bench, he sat and watched a mallard mother lead a string of half-grown ducklings downstream. Spring was moving on. He thought about mother-love—and Caroline. In her zeal to protect her son, she had almost murdered him. Charlie's comment came back to him: "You've never had any kids, have you, Fenimore?"

He remembered a play he had seen a long time ago—*The Winslow Boy*. It was about a boy who was accused of stealing a postal order. The boy's father risks their modest savings and the ruin of the family to clear the boy's name. The play is not about theft, however. It is about honor. A word seldom used today. In the end, the lawyer who clears the boy's name, explains that *right*, not justice—as defined by the letter of the law—has been done. Justice is easy. Right is hard, he explains.

Shall I forget the whole thing?

Rafferty's scowling face rose before him. *Taking the law into your own hands, Fenimore?*

A shell glided past, casting its slim shadow on the water. Such a peaceful sight. Fenimore turned away. He would call Rafferty in the morning and tell him his suspicions. Sunday was a day of rest.

EPILOGUE

When Fenimore came into the office Monday morning, Mrs. Doyle handed him four pink message slips in the order in which they arrived. Mrs. Henderson's was on top:

> Boathouse Row has been officially registered as a
> national historic landmark! Shall we have a drink to it?
>> Your Prime Suspect,
>> Myra

The next one was from the Department of Human Services:

> We would like to set up an appointment to discuss
> the whereabouts of Tanya Gonzalez at your earliest
> convenience.
>> Ms. Stephanie Patterson, Senior Case Consultant

Next—from Jennifer:

> I'll be out of town again this weekend. Take care.
>> Jen

And finally—from Rafferty:

I have some questions about that drowning yesterday.
Can you make dinner tonight at the Raven?

Raff

Fenimore lined up the slips on his desk in no particular order.
He closed the door to his inner office. He reached for the dusty
bottle of scotch (which wasn't as dusty as usual because it had
been used recently). Then, although it was barely ten o'clock, he
poured himself a stiff shot.